OVER MY DEAD BODY

When Samuel Bishop, President of Acme Electronics, hires private-investigator Brock Devlin to look into the strange behaviour and disappearance of Victor Hartman, the brilliant head of research at Acme, Bishop's concern seems understandable – especially when Devlin discovers what his client has not told him : that Hartman is his son. Devlin's investigation soon leads him to Hartman, who is involved in an affair with Yvonne Huffaker and is a badly disturbed man. The detective's intuition that all is not well deepens as the shocks along the way multiply – a disappearing ex-wife, a vanishing car, unexplained attacks, suicide and double murder. The tragedy of Hartman and Yvonne Huffaker is only part of Devlin's personal nightmare. His thirteenth case teaches him the hard way never to trust appearances – or clients – in a world where the shortest distance between desire and attainment is the double-cross.

OVER MY DEAD BODY

SCOTT MITCHELL

ROBERT HALE & COMPANY
63 Old Brompton Road, London, S.W.7

© *Scott Mitchell 1974*
First published in Great Britain 1974

ISBN 0 7091 4492 X

PRINTED IN GREAT BRITAIN BY
WILLMER BROTHERS LIMITED, BIRKENHEAD

'He who wishes to write
down his dream must be very
much awake.'

ROLAND-MANUEL

Chapter One

From the start, I didn't like the case, which went neither as I wanted it to nor as I expected it to.

I woke early and listened for a while to the gentle aubade of Kay's breathing—soft, but with a shallowness that carried hints of the new day. Raising myself on one elbow, I leaned over to inspect her. Her red hair was so long that it cascaded over the pillow. I didn't believe in a beauty that defied age : time would get us all in the end—the Cary Grants, Dietrichs and Kay Stillmans along with the John and Jane Does. But I would have made book that Kay, who had looked thirty in her early twenties, would still look thirty when she was forty. Her beauty had few points of reference to fashion or to the stereotypes of a particular decade. She wasn't concerned with being either young or mature, and her loveliness relied on no synthetic ingredients.

As I often did, I gazed at her with a kind of wonder at the improbable chemistry that had included me in her life. Years before when she had been working on her early books, she had been secretary and den-mother to Al Brody and me—a couple of characters from a dime-novel, one of whom was tough and vulgar, gloriously the real McCoy, while the other worked at it. Those were the days when I sleuthed, drank, chased girls and chewed my fingernails. Later, I gave up chewing my fingernails. I used to wonder what Kay saw in Al and me, half deciding her literary curiosity was excited by our colourful personalities—about as garish as Hollywood and Vine by night. After a while, I had another miracle on which to lavish my speculation: she was in love with me. It was the sort of alliance about which your friends (I had none) said it wouldn't work and your admirers (Kay had quite a few) said they would give it six months. The hell with that. We were still together six years later, and while it was easy to understand what I saw in her, it was more difficult to guess what she saw in me—maybe a questionable addiction to honesty and a lonely pride that was more vice than virtue, more punch-line of an old joke than subject for a noble poem. Yes, she saw that, and my bad temper, my fondness for ancient movies, my scepticism, the fragmentary education I fought hard to conceal, and my lack of money, hopes or plans.

And my need.

I kissed her gently into wakefulness, knowing that the condition would probably be a hiatus rather than the end of sleep, because Kay could surface and submerge again —a feat I had admired as a trick until I realized it was as much beyond her control as my own often paper-thin somnolence. I was a creature of light sleep and tense, spectacular awakenings from which there was seldom any return.

We had watched the late, late show in bed because I wanted to catch up on a movie I'd never seen before. She needed the extra rest.

'Hi,' I said. 'You fell asleep.'

'I usually do.' For the millionth time, I tried to gauge the elusive shade of those lambent eyes. 'After you've made love to me.'

'Maybe so, but I didn't make love to you—I'm sorry to say.'

'Oh? Oh, yes. The movie—*The Rain People*. I fell asleep, huh?'

'You were wise. It was a bummer.'

'That bad? I suppose you watched to the end.'

I nodded. 'I like punishment.'

'And lonely vigils, private pleasures. . . .' She smiled wisely. 'What time is it?'

'Eight. You go back to sleep now. Unless you could use some coffee—'

'No. You're leaving me?'

'I have a client to see. I'll call you later, princess.'

'Do that. And I hope he's a nice client.'

'They discontinued that model in 1965.'

I kissed her shoulders, covered them with the sheet and left her burrowing into the lingering warmth where my body had been.

As I showered and dressed, I thought about my nine

o'clock appointment at the office. Or not that, exactly—
rather the present stage of my career. Without desperation, I needed my prospective client, whether he wanted
me to track down a lost poodle or to prise a blackmailer
off his back. I wanted some continuity to put behind me a
bad episode that might not have damaged my confidence
but just might, in some quarters, have done nothing for
my reputation.

A month previously, I had taken a case that had
turned sour in the worst way. I had emerged with my life
and my license to operate, but not much more. As always,
I had played the hand that was dealt me (as though a
PI could do anything else). That was the trouble with
my profession: you had to take from your clients, often at
face-value, so many lies, evasions, half-truths and subter-
fuges that you were lucky if one or two of them didn't
sooner or later blow up in your face.

Temporarily, my luck had run out. My client had
turned out to be a murderess who had used me to finger
her victim. I nailed her for it, turned her in to the law,
but I didn't like being used, I didn't like the sense of
having slipped up, and most of all I hated the feeling
that I was in some way responsible for the victim's death.

The anonymous Mr Smith I was seeing after my eggs
and java might help by handing me the sort of case I
could wrap up between reading the mail and my coffee-
break.

I drove to the office, looked through a pile on my desk
that was mainly junk and dictated one quick reply to Sue

Garner. Nine o'clock came and went. Punctuality wasn't Mr Smith's strong suit. Maybe he wouldn't show. Sometimes they didn't; sometimes their problems evaporated or occasionally clients were too bashful to discuss their private matters with a PI who hadn't been shocked since Santa Claus turned out to be a phoney.

At five after nine, the telephone rang.

'This is Mr Smith.' The voice was as anonymous as the name. 'I'm sorry to change our plans, Devlin, but for several reasons, I prefer not to visit your office.'

'There's no extra charge for house-calls,' I commented.

'No, that won't do, either. Let me suggest a rendezvous.'

He told me of a drive-in and coffee-shop at Wilshire and Lincoln.

'I know it,' I said.

'How soon can you be there?'

'Ten minutes or so.'

'Fine. In that case, I'll see you—'

'Just a moment. How will I know you?'

'You won't, Devlin. Don't worry. You'll be contacted.'

He disconnected before I could tell him how much I hated mysteries.

I sighed. I took out my .38 from a desk-drawer, and as I was loading it up. Sue Garner walked in on me, her pretty eyes opening wider at what she saw.

She was a tall brunette who had replaced Kay Stillman at a time when it had seemed Kay was through

11

—and not merely as my secretary.[1] I had never looked at her as I had once looked at Kay, but Al Brody had pointed out that Sue was a pleasant sight when fluency eluded him during dictation. Al's lechery no doubt found some sort of challenge—if only theoretically—in her innocence, but he was right about her looks, and her lack of experience was maybe a salutary reminder of a younger, less jaded world.

She said, 'Was that your nine-o'clock appointment who called?'

I nodded, sliding a holster on to my belt. 'It seems he's coy of coming up here, so he's dreamed up something fancy to stimulate my interest.'

'Is that why your carrying heat?'

I laughed. 'You've got the vernacular right, honey, but I've told you before—it doesn't suit you.'

'You didn't answer my question.'

'You're an observant girl. You should have noticed by now that the occasions are getting rarer when I go out naked.'

'You think there's something wrong?'

'No. I'm sniffing at possibilities, that's all.' I smiled at the gravity that could mistake caution for a presentiment of danger. 'It's a hangover from my youth—I always hated blind-dates.'

In circumstances like those, speculation was useless, so I just drove, trying to concentrate on other matters. When I reached the drive-in, there was a mere sprinkling

[1] *See* Double Bluff

of customers—two or three business-types snatching a late breakfast on the way to the office, a girl in a battered sports-job who devoured a hamburger with a studied relish that suggested it might be her only meal that day, a middle-aged couple in a tired Ford who, unless I missed my guess, had been driving all night. A solitary man sitting in a four-door Plymouth claimed my attention briefly, if only because the make of car was favoured by the police.

But I didn't see anybody who I really thought might be Smith.

Nuts, I told myself. How did I know? If the guy was that cagey, he could have been masquerading as one of the interchangeable business-types.

A girl appeared to take my order. At least, the mini-skirt, luscious thighs and deep cleavage said girl. The face was something else. Prematurely aged by bitterness, it spoke of anxious hopes, prolonged uncertainty and final disillusionment. Without even stenographic skills, she had probably come from some upstate farm to founder in the big city where the dreams wore thin.

I ordered coffee and sat back, wondering what the next move would be. Or whose.

The coffee arrived. I had already taken a sip before I noticed the slip of paper that had been concealed under the cup. I unfolded it.

The printing on it said: 'Black Mercedes'.

Chapter Two

My first reaction was that it didn't make sense. If there had been a black Mercedes, I would have spotted it.

It simply wasn't there.

Taking another look, I saw it—about four slots down from where I sat in my Olds. It must have pulled in during the last forty-five seconds—no sooner. I couldn't see inside, because the windows were tinted.

I took a breath. Although I couldn't have said I liked the cloak-and-dagger aura, this was a smooth operation.

Crumpling up the message and putting it in my pocket, I climbed out of my heap and strolled unhurriedly to the Mercedes. At my approach, a stocky guy with oversized muscles and a face to match climbed out from in back of the wheel. He looked professionally alert without being intelligent—the sort of quality an employer sought in hired muscle, in whom being smart could be as much a liability as an asset.

All depending on the employer and how much he had to conceal.

Nodding to me, the stocky guy opened the rear door at precisely the right moment, and from inside, well hidden by shadows I failed to penetrate, the sun being in my eyes, a metallic voice said, 'Get in, Devlin. I apologize for the touch of melodrama.'

'That's all right,' I said. 'Life *is* melodrama. They tame it down for television.'

I swung myself on the rear seat. The stocky guy closed the door, climbed smartly into the front and half turned his head, having already started the motor, for his master's instructions.

'Take off, Harry,' his master said. 'Just ride us around.'

I took a look at the man issuing the orders. He was grizzled, in his late sixties or early seventies, and he wore a blue business-suit. As he was sitting down, it was hard to tell, but I thought he was probably tall. He was certainly slim, with gaunt, almost emaciated features, the most arresting being a surgical slit for a mouth. I couldn't see his eyes for intensely dark shades, and that bothered me—that and the tinted glass of the Mercedes. The face, however, was that of an aristocrat. If physiognomy had any meaning at all, those features spoke of austere disdain, perhaps even of refined cruelty.

His voice revealed patrician hauteur, too, as he said, 'I like your attitude, Devlin.'

'That's a novelty. I hope I don't disappoint you.'

'We'll see.' His smile would not have thawed even a small ice-cube. 'For a start, you obey orders—'

'They were scarcely worth disobeying, Mr Smith—if that's your real name, and I can't believe it is—'

'Prosaic, you mean? Sound intuition. I am Samuel Bishop, and the alias, I confess, was expedient rather than imaginative. Have you heard of me?'

'To a prospective client, I'd like to say yes. But I'd be a liar.'

He nodded. 'There's no reason why you should have heard of me. More precisely, since I spend large sums doing exactly the opposite of publicising myself, there are good reasons why I should be unknown to you. Anonymity has its attractions, especially in this gaudy age, and today's secrecy was by no means uncharacteristic.'

'I understand.'

He left me some silence to chew on before he remarked, 'You're a patient man.'

'Don't make book on it. It's professional and cultivated —not temperamental. Besides, I figure sooner or later we're going to get to what's in the bottom of the pail.'

'Good thinking. Well, Devlin, I control Acme Electronics, a large and important Los Angeles corporation whose name just might be familiar to you. We're into space research in a big way—most of it work for the federal government and consequently highly secret. When I say I control Acme, I don't mean that I go there every day and sit myself down behind a desk. There are periods during which I don't go near the place in weeks, and I have other interests, equally demanding of my time and energies. That means I must

17

employ people whom I trust. One of the most important of these is Victor Hartman, who is in charge of Acme's research programme. Are you making any sense of this so far?'

'It begins to add up, Mr Bishop. I guess you're narrowing your focus.'

'Exactly. Let's talk about Victor Hartman. He's in his late forties—a brilliant man with three degrees from two European universities. Victor joined Acme fifteen years ago, but I knew him before then, and I may say he's been like a son to me. He has an astonishing mind—inventive, original, questing, and not limited merely to theory. My satisfaction in him has been enormous.'

I said nothing to that, perhaps because I had no son and I didn't intend to have one. I speculated, though, whether I, in Bishop's place, would have placed the same value on such cerebral qualities.

My prospective client went on, 'For a scientist, Victor has a near-ideal temperament. He's deliberate, methodical and objective in a way that can't be cultivated—only inborn. I speak from experience, Devlin—bitter experience. I've known men who were undeniably brilliant, but also flashy and volatile, the kind who would rush to judgment at the expense of the one small detail that would vitiate their findings. In Victor Hartman, however, I had supreme confidence.'

'Why the past tense?'

'You offer me a cue?' His thin smile was a grimace. 'You know your trade—or at least this stage of it—and I appreciate that. About six months ago, Victor divorced his wife, Deborah. After twenty years of marriage, it seemed almost a superfluous action. So far as I know, neither of them had lovers, and neither could have accused the other of anything worse than familiarity. The truth is, I suppose, that the relationship had worn out. Like fatigue in metal, staleness had corrupted the marriage. Maybe that's what we all have to fear in the end—unspectacular dissolution, creeping death. Don't believe what they tell you about holocausts and cataclysms. Daily erosion is the enemy.' He grunted pessimistically. 'Bear with my philosophical asides, Devlin. I haven't lost the thread.'

'I didn't suppose you had. You seem like a man who knows exactly what he's saying.'

'Thank you for that—if it's a compliment. Well, Victor appeared to survive the divorce quite convincingly. He didn't confide in me, but his reasons for it were no doubt positive. The need for greater urgency in life and so on. I guess you could say that he and Deborah both were cleaning house.'

'And yet, after twenty years, divorce should have its traumatic aspects. Unless, for motives I can't guess, you haven't told me the truth.'

'That's a perceptive comment. But I have told you the truth. I think the break hit Victor hard, but his surface remained intact for some time.'

'Until when?'

'Almost a month ago. I hadn't seen him in weeks, but

19

when he came to dinner one evening, it was easy—the more so because of the gap—to spot that he was jumpy, worried and depressed.'

'And you found that unusual?'

'Wouldn't you?'

'No, it's a twentieth-century condition. Most of the folk I meet are jumpy, worried and depressed.'

The dark lenses swivelled my way for a moment as if to comment that I took one hell of a bleak view of life.

I wouldn't have denied that.

Then he said, 'It was unusual for Victor Hartman—you must take it from me. I attributed his condition to a delayed response to the ending of his life with Deborah—that, and the difficulties inevitably facing a man on his own after so many years.'

I smiled. 'You mean girls. Forgive my being so basic.'

'Do I mean girls? All right, I guess I do—though only in part. Victor is a sociable man, he has a number of friends, and divorced people are no longer regarded as cripples in our society.'

'Is he seeing a woman?' I persisted.

'I wouldn't know, though I suspect Deborah might. Even when their husbands are no longer their husbands, women have antennae for that sort of thing.'

'What about work? Could Hartman have hit a rock with something he was working on?'

'I don't think so. You must understand his function, which, to a high degree, is administrative—probably more so than he, pre-eminent in his field, would prefer.

20

Victor heads up a team, you see. He directs and co-ordinates, coaxes forth the best individual talents of the members of that team and oversees the whole current research-project.'

'And what is that?'

He smiled patronisingly. 'Even if I could tell you, I wouldn't. All such projects are top-secret. But I have no impulse to tell you. I know Victor, and it wasn't his work that was bothering him.'

'You say you know him. But by implication you haven't seen much of him recently.'

'That's true, but don't attach too much weight to it. Victor may have his secrets—private corners of his life, but my knowledge of him is deep. Work wasn't what was preying on his mind that night. I asked him whether he would like a vacation.'

'Then he's not indispensable?'

'Nobody is indispensable.'

'What did he say?'

'He turned me down. That was the last time I saw him. However, a week later, he called me and said he wanted to take me up on the offer. A courtesy-call, you understand—Victor could arrange for leave of absence at any time without consulting me. I may control Acme Electronics, but not, as I told you, by sitting in an office on the top floor.'

'How long did he plan on being away?' I asked, guessing what was coming.

'If you mean away in the sense of travelling or leaving

town—he didn't. But he said I was right, he'd reached a certain pitch of exhaustion, and three weeks' leave would be welcome. I repeated my concern and asked him to have dinner with me again. The invitation was for five days ago. But Victor never arrived that night. There was no explanation, no apology—merely an unexplained absence so uncharacteristic of the man that it worried me, so much so that, having failed to reach him by telephone, I tried to see him. His rent is paid up until the end of the month, but his clothes are gone. He's left his apartment.'

'But the rent is paid. He could be coming back.'

'It's possible.'

'Is he in LA?'

'I suspect so.'

'Who might know where he is?'

'Deborah, his wife. Or ex-wife—it's hard to think of them apart. Anyway, she's living in Ventura.' He grimaced—it seemed a little trick of his, some unsuspected symptom of fleeting disgust, though at whom or what it was hard to tell. 'As you have probably divined by now, I want you to find Victor Hartman for me.'

'Yes, it began to stack up that way.' I thought matters over. 'Outfits like yours tend to keep pretty close tabs. Furthermore, your tie-in with federal agencies isn't hard to imagine. Couldn't your own security-people find him?'

'No doubt they could—and at the same time raise precisely the sort of hue and cry I want to avoid. But that's not the point. Forget Acme, Devlin. My concern is personal, and my commission is relatively simple. Yes,

I want you to find Victor for me—that part, I suspect, shouldn't be too difficult for you. When you've done that, however, I want you also to discover what he's doing, where he goes, whom he's seeing. No more than that.'

'And no less than that,' I pointed out. 'Item: if he's disappeared, if he's pulled down the curtain, he could be tough to find—not to say impossible. Item: even if I find him, a guy like Hartman, a genius or near-genius as you describe him, is hard to shadow successfully.'

'I'll take the second objection first. Victor may not be the absent-minded-professor type, but he's scarcely going to anticipate surveillance. As for his disappearance, I don't think that's exactly sinister or elaborate—he's simply chosen to drop out of circulation for a while.'

'Why?'

'He has problems. We've discussed that.'

'And what's your motive in this? I have to ask that question. I want to be very sure I understand.'

He sighed. 'I'm not an emotional man, Devlin. Or at least I don't show my feelings—I have an exaggerated respect for discipline. But Victor and I were once very close. I'd hate to fail him now just because he hasn't cried out for help.'

'Maybe he doesn't need it.'

'Maybe not. Nevertheless, I'd like to assess the situation for myself. Hence my need for your services.'

I rapidly sized up the proposition. If there were parts of it I didn't like, that was par for the course: every commission had its loose ends and jagged edges. But if

23

there were aspects of larceny to this one, I couldn't spot them. Bishop's attitude was paternalisitic, even offensively imbued with do-goodery; but it seemed genuine enough.

Though Samuel Bishop was not an easy man to figure. The shades he wore were symbolic—typical LA shutters over the windows of the soul.

'I'll take the case,' I said. 'How long do I have?'

'If you can't locate Victor within four days or at least turn up something, then his absence, should he fail to return to work, becomes official and will be investigated automatically because of the security-angle. Let's see what you can do during those four days.'

'Since you've touched on the subject, could Hartman have been kidnapped?'

'It's most unlikely, Devlin. I take it you're thinking along political lines. Well, Victor's mind might be useful to an enemy if he could be persuaded to co-operate, but the popular notion of scientists as walking repositories of secret formulae is pretty wide of the mark, you know. No, Victor might be in trouble, but the brand of trouble I have in mind is the spiritual crisis of a man who's reached the end of his tether.'

There was even more flexible steel in my client's tones —a patronizing edge that irritated me in its suggestion that my lurid imaginings were immature, comic-book stuff.

Anticipating the answer, I asked him whether I could talk to people at the plant.

'No,' he said. 'Once you do that, the whole thing is out in the open, and I'd find it tough to prevent it passing out of my hands entirely. If you're thinking of colleagues, though, Victor has a close friend who was with Acme until a year ago. They still keep in touch, I believe. His name is Ben Craddock and he teaches at UCLA now. You'll have no trouble finding his address. Then there's Deborah—I imagine you'll want to talk to her.' He gave me the address in Ventura.

Afterwards we talked about the inevitable topic, and the sum he gave me for a retainer was more than satisfactory.

Perhaps a little strange, too, in its generosity. Bishop hadn't even asked me what the going-rate was for this type of work.

Maybe he already knew and had made up his mind to pay over it. Just as maybe, behind those opaque shades, there was a detailed knowledge of Brock Devlin and his talents. I wondered who or what had made him pick on me.

But I didn't ask.

When I asked how I would reach him, however, he gave me a telephone number.

'That's all I'm giving you,' he added. 'You're smart. You could easily find out my address, but if you come calling, you better have a damned good reason. That goes for the telephone. Don't use it unless your information can't wait.'

'Then how do we keep in touch?'

25

'I'll call you.'

I shrugged, indulgent of his quirks, and his grimace was there again. At first, I thought he was showing his disdain for my approval or disapproval, but the grimace intensified until it spread his mouth and seemed to devour his whole face in a kind of silent scream. He tilted forward, and his fingers, immaculately manicured and expensively beringed, twisted in towards his palms like talons.

'What's wrong?' I asked.

'Nothing.' The metal in his voice was a rasp now. 'Nothing.' He took a deep breath, sitting up with an effort. 'At least nothing you or anybody else can do anything about. You're looking at a dying man, Devlin. I have cancer of the stomach—the death-sentence. Pain and I are old friends—old enemies, at least. Pain you don't come to terms with, though you may cheat it at the expense of life itself.'

The opulence of the Mercedes was suddenly doing nothing to dissipate the impression of mortality. As well as the smell of expensive leather, I inhaled despair and rage. The man I was riding with was staring at a blank wall.

'I'm sorry,' I said.

'Fine.' His smile was sardonic. 'I'll take your pity if it urges you to work harder finding that boy.'

He got in touch with Harry and told him to head back for the drive-in. On the return-trip, we said almost nothing.

26

Over My Dead Body

The Mercedes had completed the round-trip before I realized that I had not asked Bishop for a picture of Victor Hartman. The oversight was a near-unprecedented lapse, but perhaps my excuse was Bishop's revelation of his losing battle with Big C. Since, as it turned out, he had predictably come prepared, I asked myself why he, too, had forgotten about the picture. Maybe the truth on his side was that, like a man encountering reality afresh by articulating it to a stranger, he had momentarily been stunned.

The photograph, a glossy ten-by-eight, showed that Hartman had the lean, boyish good-looks of a John F. Kennedy, though the smile, with its hints of sadness, evoked Bobby rather than John. I wondered whether those attributes had been as useful in the electronics industry as they had in getting votes. Probably not. They were the sort of looks, even so, that women went for in large numbers—a conclusion of importance to me inasmuch as Hartman's personal life would no doubt turn out to be at least as much my concern as his career.

I climbed out of the black Mercedes, which took off leaving me blinking in the abrupt glare of the sunlight from which I had been insulated in the darkened, air-conditioned car.

Even to a man used to strange circumstances, the episode was bizarre, so that with the Mercedes gone, I might have asked myself whether I had dreamed up the whole thing.

But the bills in my pocket were real enough.

27

Chapter Three

I started with Dr Benjamin Craddock, drawing a blank on campus, where they told me I should find him at home. They were right. His apartment was conveniently close to the campus, and he opened the door to me himself—a delicately featured man, with irritable, spastic movements and, behind steel-framed eyeglasses, black and round hyperthalmic eyes. He was dressed casually in short-sleeved shirt, tan slacks and loafers, but the garb, in true Los Angeles style, was misleading, for his wasn't company, I guessed immediately, to relax in.

A hi-fi was blaring Beethoven's Emperor Concerto in the room into which he showed me, a room heavy with anonymity and airlessness, its solemnity established principally by yards of books, big lamps with shades like umbrellas and several black leather chairs. Craddock had invited me in offhandedly and without hesitation, as though PI's frequently called on him, but his manner bugged me from the start: it was supercilious, aloof, civil without being courteous, and he made no move to turn down the music, over which it was going to be tough to talk.

'What's on your mind, Mr Devlin?' he asked.

Pitching my voice louder than I liked, I explained, 'I'm anxious to locate Victor Hartman, who I believe is a friend of yours. But he seems kind of hard to reach right now.'

'That so?'

He showed no surprise or heightening of interest.

'You *are* a friend of his?' I said.

'Oh, yes. Now what would a private investigator want with Victor?'

'I'm afraid I can't tell you that. It's confidential.'

'Well, have it your way.'

He looked bored, his eyes sliding away from me and his fingers drumming as though he would soon dismiss me and rush off to other, more absorbing tasks. I was getting nowhere with him. He was handing me a kind of bland non-co-operation, passive resistance. Furthermore, the pounding Beethoven was beginning to rattle my composure.

I decided to try a confidence trick—or finesse, as we called it in the trade.

Almost yelling to top the racket, I said, 'That's pretty impressive—Richter, I'd imagine.'

Craddock fell for it. He was a culture vulture, a transparent intellectual snob.

His mouth opened, and he blinked three times before a slow smile announced the dawn. We had exchanged signals in the night, and now all was well. Leaping up, he turned down the hi-fi to near vanishing-point.

'You like the Emperor?' he asked.

I flashed him a few more signals. 'Well, if I'm honest, I prefer the Fourth.'

It was a subtle lie or half-truth. The truth was that while I preferred the Fourth Concerto to the Emperor, I had no special fondness for Beethoven, and when Kay, in a blessedly uncharacteristic fit of missionary zeal, had tried to get me hooked on the mighty man of music, we had had fierce, sometimes bitter arguments. As for the soloist, my nominating Richter had been a gambler's play.

But I was right, and it brought the house down.

'Well, I'm damned,' Craddock declared. 'You're a queer fish for a private dick.'

'Listen,' I said, 'don't hand me the Congressional Medal. Everybody knows Ludwig these days. The pop-music boys have frisked him for new tunes—but good.'

He laughed. 'Don't give me that, Devlin. Everybody doesn't recognize Richter when he hears him.'

'Well, don't let this get out. It would ruin my standing with several cops I know.'

'Your secret is safe with me. You say you want to find Victor Hartman? You know where he lives, of course?'

'Yes, but he seems to be away—temporarily.'

'Then I'm afraid I'm not going to be much help to you. I can't suggest where he might be.'

'That's a pity. I had hoped—'

31

'It's true Victor and I are friends, but not if you reckon it by the amount of time we spend together. I haven't seen him for weeks. There was a time when we were closer, but that was in the days when we were both working for Acme Electronics.'

'What made you quit?'

He snorted. 'I'd had it. The material rewards were good, of course, but the pressure was on, and the academic life began to look more and more attractive. Besides, in a political sense—and I use the term in its broadest application—I was a non-starter. I'd offended a few people and promotion wasn't about to come my way —even if I'd asked Victor to use his influence. And I wouldn't have done that.'

'But Hartman did all right?'

'Better than all right. It's a funny thing—I hated him at first, thought there was something creepy about him. We're going back a few years now, of course, to a time when Sam Bishop was actively the presiding force at Acme. He still pulls the strings, but from a distance. I hear he's not a well man.'

At his interrogative glance, I said evasively, 'Yes, I have the same impression.'

Unpredictably, Craddock laughed. 'Sam Bishop— SB, they call him. Except for those of us who hate his guts, and we call him SOB, because that's what he is. He's an old-fashioned autocrat of the worst kind—that is, he loves you so long as your preoccupations coincide with his preoccupations. If they don't, watch out. Well,

Victor used to be his shadow. Everywhere the SOB went, there was Victor, and if Bishop did the talking, you had the feeling that Victor Hartman supplied the thoughts and information. I can tell you it was kind of sinister.'

'But you changed your opinion of Hartman?'

'Oh, yes. Victor's all right. A little intense, maybe, but that's the kind of climate Acme generates—one of my reasons for quitting. He tried to persuade me there was a different, more sympathetic side to the old man, but I never felt the urge to find out for myself. There's no doubt Victor lets the old man dominate him.' He regarded me with a measure of scepticism. 'I don't know what your business is with Victor, and I don't know whether all this is helping you, but while I guess I'm a compulsive talker, I wouldn't tell you if I didn't believe you could get the same information easily enough from other sources.'

'I understand. But let's try stepping into slightly more private ground. What happened to Hartman's marriage?'

'Even if I wanted to, I couldn't tell you a lot about that. I think there were problems on both sides. I'm a bachelor—a student of marriage from the outside. One of my conclusions is that it can start out well, become a habit and then become a drag once you realize it's become a habit.'

'And that happened to Deborah and Victor Hartman?'

'That—and other things. Deborah drinks a lot these days. She used to be an attractive woman, but alcohol can be a sort of monomania, I guess, boring to others. It tends to shove things aside, including genuinely appealing qualities. Then Victor became a very disillusioned man in recent years.'

'Disillusioned? About what?'

'Oh, all the big questions, Devlin. Life, the way this country is run—even, perhaps, his work, though Victor is pretty naive about that. When your eyes are focused so narrowly, it's easy not to take in the whole scene.' He leaned back in his chair and grinned disarmingly. 'Have I helped you, Devlin?'

'I beg your pardon?'

'You say you'd like to talk to Victor—'

'I said I want to find him.'

'You're pretty interested in him—as what?'

'As a source of information. Look, I'd tell you more if I could, but—'

'Save it. A private dick who digs Beethoven is still a private dick. You're not about to tell me the real nature of your business, so spare me the phoney stories. I'm certain Victor has nothing to hide.'

Automatically, I said, 'I'm sure he hasn't.'

'Well, where do you go from here? Acme?'

'No, I've already checked—Hartman has taken a vacation. I may try talking to Deborah Hartman.'

'Deborah?' Craddock frowned. 'Is she still in town? I understood she'd gone back East, where she came from.'

'She's not in town exactly. She's living out at Ventura.'

'No kidding. You surprise me. I was pretty sure she'd gone back East.'

'Not if my information is reliable.'

'Well, I wish you luck. Deborah used not to be the talkative type, but that was before she hit the bottle.'

'A laconic lush—that would be a novelty.'

Craddock looked uncomfortable. 'I didn't exactly say she was a lush, Devlin.' He shrugged. 'Oh, it's the truth, I guess. If I'm a little reluctant to face it, the explanation is that they were both good friends of mine. One of the features I hate about divorce is that when the split finally comes, you so often have to choose which partner you're going to stay friendly with.'

Since the interview was clearly over, I stood up. Craddock did likewise and turned up the just audible Beethoven. The finale was in full swing, crammed with the recapitulations that turned me off—especially when I hadn't much cared for the first statement of the musical material.

Craddock gestured towards the speakers. 'I quit Acme to have more time to enjoy this sort of thing. Victor is totally committed, you know. That's his business, but I believe no man should make so lavish an investment. Not to electronics or to anything else.'

We said goodbye, and I liked him better than I had at first. There was something attractively immature about him, as though he were a sophomore belatedly stumbling over a few truisms and thinking nobody else had hit on them before.

As I left the apartment-house, somebody on the street took off at speed in a four-door Plymouth, accelerating so hard that the tyres complained noisily. I couldn't see who was behind the wheel, but the colour was identical to that of the Plymouth I had seen earlier.

Coincidences happened, but this time I made a note of the licence-number.

Chapter Four

Despite the one or two points I had to think over, my drive out of LA on the Ventura Freeway was uneventful and boring.

Perhaps not wishing to talk myself out of a job, I had not discussed with Samuel Bishop what would happen when I began asking around after Hartman. No matter how discreet, any PI was likely to kick up a dust that his quarry could see from twenty miles.

Especially if those to whom he talked began lifting telephones.

I thought about Ben Craddock. He, certainly, might have tipped off Victor Hartman, but I had the impression that, unless he was a better liar than he seemed, he didn't know where Hartman was—if one assumed, as my client clearly did, that Hartman had moved out of his apartment. Even if Craddock did warn his friend, though, my job would not necessarily be made impossible unless Hartman wanted to run.

Craddock's surprise at the whereabouts of Deborah

Hartman suggested he would not, on the other hand, be talking to her. Ventura was a fair ride, so that I considered warning her myself of my visit but decided against it. If I found her not at home, I might have to kick around, but at least she wouldn't be prepared, having been given chance to think about my call and rehearse her answers.

The address Bishop has supplied led me to an English-style bungalow at the dead end of a one-block cul-de-sac. I was in luck. The door was opened by Deborah Hartman herself, an elegantly tall woman of about forty, wearing black sweater and pants that seemed more formal on her than conventional garb would have done. Her dark hair was swept upwards in an effect that flirted with severity, since her features were not generous but rather sculpted to a fine point at which delicacy almost trespassed upon austerity. She had pretty eyes, though, pellucidly blue, and they helped counteract the impression created by a mouth that turned down unattractively at the corners in a way that reminded me of Jeanne Moreau. Her general bearing, particularly her manner of holding her head, announced a woman who was accustomed if not to dominating situations then seldom allowing them to slip from her grasp.

She looked a toughie, I thought, and if her heart had hardened towards her ex-husband, I wondered what I was going to get out of her but abuse.

Introducing myself, I gave her one of my cards, which she studied before she asked me in. She seemed to have trouble reading it. Maybe she normally wore eyeglasses to read. Or since it was by now early afternoon, maybe the day was far enough advanced for Deborah Hartman's vision to be blurred.

She showed me into a living room whose glass and tubular steel furniture evoked Scandinavia and created an agreeably clinical impression diluted by luxurious rugs made from black and white sheepskins. The room had order and discipline. If its mistress was a lush, her addiction didn't reveal itself in sloppy housekeeping.

I sat on an arrangement of steel and plastic that was a damned sight more comfortable than it looked. It had to be.

Deborah Hartman sat opposite me and studied me with a mixture of critical intelligence and undisguised amusement.

'You're anxious to talk to my ex-husband?' Her voice was low and faintly husky, possibly her best attribute. 'What about?'

'I'm afraid I can't discuss that. Actually, I simply said I wanted to trace him.'

'Why? Is he missing?'

I made a mental note to watch my step. 'Not missing exactly. Just somewhat—elusive.'

'Did he skip a couple of payments on his car? Are you working for a finance-company?'

'When I play twenty questions, I usually ask the questions. Besides, you're not serious. I detect a satirical edge.'

39

'Bravo,' she said softly. 'You're at least alert, Mr Devlin.'

'Since you mentioned his car, what make does he drive?'

'A white Aston-Martin. Probably because it runs counter to the stereotype of a stuffy scientist.' She frowned. 'But I don't get this. Where is Victor? I spoke to him recently—only a couple of days ago.'

'You did? What about?'

'He called me about a couple of legal loose-ends. You know we're divorced?'

I nodded. 'Did he seem normal?'

'I'm not sure I understand that question. He seemed like Victor. Why shouldn't he?'

'No reason. I would like to talk to him, though.'

'Isn't he at his apartment?'

'No—seemingly not. Also he's on vacation from work.'

'Then he could be anywhere.'

'Perhaps so. I was hoping you could help me.'

'Perhaps I can.'

She glanced uneasily at me. In fact, her gaze kept flickering off to one side in a manner that seemed almost dishonest until I realized that her eyes were continually drawn to an empty tumbler standing on a low, glass-topped table.

I thought I understood what that was all about.

She said slowly, 'I can guess who hired you.'

'Can you?'

'Sure—Sam Bishop. You're not going to deny knowing

40

Sam Bishop, are you?'

'No. I won't deny that. I admit having talked to him. Victor is a subject of concern with him. I gather he feels about him as another man might feel about his son.'

'Is that what the old rogue said?' Deborah Hartman laughed bitterly, incredulously. 'Do you believe everything you hear, Mr Devlin?'

'About half—on my philanthropic days.'

Her eyes—they were really much lovelier than their setting—shone captivatingly.

'I think I like you,' she said. 'Would you care for a drink?'

'If it would help you.'

'You know it would help me, you cynical bastard. You've done your research. Well, what will it be?'

'Bourbon and a splash of water will do fine.'

She nodded and walked gracefully to a corner of the room where there was a miniature bar and refrigerator. Something about the way she clattered bottles and glasses sounded fake to me—as though she was not so sober as she pretended to be or—and the second explanation seemed less likely—as though she were a pro pretending to be an amateur. She had mixed booze before. I couldn't understand what all the fuss was about.

She returned with the drinks—bourbon for me, vodka for her.

I looked around the room without seeing a picture of Victor Hartman.

41

'You know,' I said, 'I don't have a photograph of your ex-husband. You couldn't help, could you?'

'Certainly. Excuse me one moment.'

She left the room, and while she was gone, I sampled my drink. It was almost pure bourbon—without sufficient water to weaken it at the knees. I took a sip from Deborah Hartman's glass, and the contrast was spectacular. The amount of vodka in there would have made a Russian die of shame and thirst. She was drinking almost unfortified water.

I didn't know what it proved, but the situation was interesting.

She came back with the picture—a small one, but, so far as I could tell, a good likeness.

'Thanks,' I said. 'It might help.'

'A lot of things might help.'

Although she was standing close to me, her proximity didn't prepare me for what followed. She pressed herself to me and kissed me on the lips, her mouth tasting clean and sweet as though she hadn't touched a drink all day— though vodka was the most elusive form of alcohol to detect on the breath. If she hadn't been tall, she would not have been able to do what she did without my co-operation.

She murmured, 'To a hungry, deprived woman, you're hellish attractive.' She laughed at the rationalizing streak in the remark. 'Damn it, to a well nourished woman, you'd still be attractive.'

She kissed me again. This time, with my glass in one

hand and Hartman's picture in the other, I backed off. At that, it wasn't a bad defence—certainly less alienating or humiliating for her than if I had pushed her away.

Disappointment rather than anger crossed her features like a shadow. 'So you don't mix business and pleasure.'

'It's not that,' I said, 'though I'd say it's a good idea for any PI not to get into bed with client's wives or the sexual partners of key figures in a case. I guess that goes for ex-partners, too.'

'Did I invite you into my bed?'

'Didn't you?'

She sighed with resignation. 'What is it, then?'

'It's personal. Nothing against you at all.'

'For a detective, you're a great diplomat.' She sat down. 'All right. Let's talk sensibly. What's happened to Victor?'

'Nothing. Not in the sense you mean. Has he been under a strain recently?'

'You forget—I'm no longer the authority. But you seem to be well informed.' She gulped her drink thirstily. Water was good for thirst. 'Sam Bishop was your source of information, I presume. You said something about Sam's fatherly feelings. That's quite a notion, Mr Devlin.'

'You repudiate the idea?'

'No, I'd just like to get it clear. What lies did Sam tell you?'

'He said he and Victor had been very close—like father and son.'

43

'Like!' She laughed scornfully. 'I have news for you, Mr Devlin, so hang on to your hat. Victor Hartman *is* Sam Bishop's son!'

That was news, all right.

I digested it in silence before I asked, 'How do you know?'

Sidestepping the question, she said, 'It's an interesting story—full of tragedy and poetry. Or, if you don't care for fine feelings, it's a rip-roaring farce. But in case you don't like tales of love, honour and betrayal, I'll keep it brief. Two men founded Acme Electronics. One was Sam Bishop and the other Karl Hartman. Hartman was the real genius, the man of science, but Bishop was the driving force, the thrust that translated Karl's dreams into reality. The two partners seemed to complement each other. By the time the firm began to thrive, both men had acquired wives—Karl's a gentle, intellectually unremarkable creature, while Sam Bishop's wife had ambitions to match Sam's own aspirations. Both Bishop and Hartman were still young, but as business boomed, Karl, who had never been exactly worldly, became even more the dreamer and withdrawn in his experiments and research. He neglected his wife or at least spent little time with her. On the other hand, Bishop probably saw too much of *his* wife—a cold fish, by all accounts, though her social climbing no doubt suited Sam well enough. In his younger days, Sam Bishop had, they tell me, a kind of charm—if you could overlook his ruthlessness, and I never could. Before long, Mary Hartman became his mistress. If Karl suspected anything at all, he kept quiet, but then Mary became pregnant. I don't know when or how Hartman decided that Sam Bishop was the father of his son Victor, but it must have been approximately a year after Victor's birth. Those who remember say Karl was oldfashioned, perhaps foolishly considerate, certainly a gentleman of the old school. There was an accident. His car ran off the road, and Karl Hartman was killed, leaving his wife and son extremely well provided for.'

'Quite a story. What's the sequel? Did Bishop eventually marry the widow?'

'No. And if Lila Bishop, his wife, guessed anything, she probably kept her ideas to herself. Lila died seven years ago, but by that time Mary Hartman was also dead.'

'How do you know all this?'

'Victor told me. On her death-bed, his mother broke the news to him.'

'And what are his feelings?'

'Complicated, but positive. Freud would have been disappointed in him, but don't forget he's known Bishop all his life and grew up regarding him as a second father. The psychological transition, when it finally came, wasn't all that difficult.'

'Who else knows this?'

'Scarcely anybody alive. And you wouldn't be favoured, Mr Devlin, if I weren't lonely, hadn't been drinking and didn't have an abiding distaste for Sam Bishop.'

45

'Thanks, anyway.'

I had two lies to think about: Bishop had carefully not told me of his true relationship to Victor Hartman; and he had described the man as an employee, which he probably wasn't in any sense that I understood the word.

I asked, 'Has you ex-husband a financial interest in Acme?'

'Yes, though it's not the large one you're probably imagining. When Victor was still a boy, Mary Hartman, who was no businesswoman, sold out her share to Sam Bishop—no doubt at his urging. Sam's a sentimental character. After Karl Hartman's death, she travelled a lot in Europe, where Victor was mainly educated. I gather the affair with Sam Bishop finished abruptly, and my guess is that she was stricken with remorse.'

I nodded. 'If it's not too personal, let's talk about your own marriage.'

'If we're going to get that personal, I could use another drink. How about you?'

'No, thanks.'

She built herself one with her back to me so that I could form no idea of the ingredients. Maybe the first one was for show, and this one would be for real.

She sat down again and said, 'I meant what I said about Sam Bishop, but I suppose I'm not simple enough to blame him for the breakdown of our marriage. If he kept Victor immersed in his work, Victor was a willing victim. He grew to neglect me as much as Karl neglected Mary Hartman. Curious how patterns repeat themselves.

46

We were rich, of course, and had a lovely house. But it was never really a home. Victor had his work, and I had—well, politics, in the end. At least, I pretended to be interested and worked at it. If you want a label, I guess I'm a left-wing Republican.'

'What about Victor's politics?'

'We had nothing to agree or argue about. Victor has no politics.'

'And they're the worst kind'—my mind gave back to me antiphonally and automatically. But I didn't say it, perhaps because the thought wasn't mine, merely some catch-phrase I had once heard uttered by a politically minded acquaintance of Kay.

Her voice thick, Deborah Hartman said, 'Maybe it would have helped if we'd had children, but my instincts weren't exactly strong, and Victor doesn't care for children. Do you?'

'Not particularly.'

'You're very polite. That sounds like a patronizing, watered-down answer.'

I was wondering what was watered down, but it wasn't my answer I had in mind.

'Very well', I said. 'For me, kids wouldn't represent fulfilment—just an impediment. Smart people don't have kids, and having them is an antisocial act. My own childhood was boring at best and lousy at worst. I see no charm or innocence in the condition. For me, it was a period to get through as fast as I could and with the least embarrassment. I haven't a scrap of fatherly feeling or longing for progeny. Is that strong enough for you?'

She nodded. 'And close to Victor's ideas, though he rarely articulated them. I suspect many men feel that way—and perhaps an equal number of women, though they're scared to admit it.'

'So what happened to your marriage?'

'We reached a point at which there was little to hold it together. But there were more positive factors. Victor finally grew conscious of missed chances in a personal sense. We married young, and he'd never known any other woman. Scholarship and research had pre-empted a sizeable chunk of his life. You might say he was experiencing the thousand small regrets that come with his age. Soul-searching, if you like. If I have bitterness, you see, it's not really towards Victor. I can't blame him, particularly as I was tired, too, in ways with which I won't bore you.'

I became aware of the passing of time and another related phenomenon—the gradual thickening and slurring of her speech.

I reminded her, 'You said perhaps you could help me.'

'I believe so. I haven't exactly been keeping tabs on Victor, but I know he's met another woman. Her name is Yvonne Huffaker, and she's married. I met her once—a pretty, shy woman, as I recall. I'm not sure where she lives, but if you're the detective I think you are, you'll find her without much trouble. When you do, my guess is that you'll be close to Victor.'

48

So Samuel Bishop's hunch had been accurate: he had seemed pretty certain that Deborah Hartman would have information of value.

I thanked her, and as I prepared to leave, I said, 'That telephone call you mentioned—did you—'

'It was quite impersonal, Mr Devlin. Business matters.'

'You don't have a number where you can reach him?'

'Apart from Acme—no, I don't. There are the lawyers, of course. He broke a long silence with that call, but twenty years of marriage leave a few loose ends, and there was one he wanted to tie off quickly.' She laughed drunkenly. 'No spectacular personal revelations, if that's what you're thinking. I ceased to be his confessor long ago. Strange how you miss these burdens. But they are burdens, so let's not get maudlin about it. I guess even slaves can miss their chains. Don't you think so?'

Just before I left, she said, 'I know Sam Bishop hired you. Don't bother to deny it. I doubt whether you know much about Sam Bishop, but just ask yourself this. What makes you so sure he has Victor's well-being at heart?'

Chapter Five

I started back for LA with her words ringing in my ears like a taunt. After a while, though, they were thrust aside by a pulse—near-subliminal, insidious, inescapable. Before I realized it was there and recognized its cause, the pulse became as loud as a drumbeat.

Twice, before I joined the freeway, I had glimpsed a tan Mustang in my rearview. A quarter-mile in back of me, the Mustang was still there.

It could have been a different tan Mustang, but intuition told me it wasn't.

Without going in for a spurt, I increased my speed steadily and then eased off. When I checked, I saw that the Mustang had kept its station—neither closer nor more distant. Again, keeping the manoeuvre as casual as I could, I switched lanes.

The Mustang did, too.

At that distance, it was hard to be sure, but I figured there were probably two men in it.

My battered Olds wasn't quite the heap it seemed. Beneath its faded hood throbbed a motor kept tuned by a near-genius with automobiles. Even so, I didn't fancy trying to outrun the Mustang, which might well have been similarly juiced-up and was a much younger car.

A sign advertising Denny's Coffee Shop flashed past, reminding me that I was close to Malibu Canyon. I hit the gas hard and streaked for the next exit.

A glance told me that the Mustang, weaving in and out among other vehicles, had taken off, too.

Audibly burning rubber, I cut back across the freeway and began to negotiate the curves of a twisting uphill road on which I expected to encounter little traffic. As I climbed, I occasionally caught sight of the Mustang below me and faintly heard the tormented screams of its tires.

I didn't give much for my chances of shaking the Mustang—the Olds handled like a barge in the tighter turns—but at least I was better off here than on the freeway.

Or worse off—depending on my luck and the intentions of my pursuers. If they caught up to me, this was pretty lonely terrain.

And they were catching up to me.

A hairpin offered me another glimpse of the tan Mustang, still below me, but gaining. The road straightened out for a downhill stretch long enough for the pursuing driver, once he had realized his opportunity, to try closing the gap. As I figured that out, I spotted a dirt road on my right with, beside it, a ramshackle sign that said it led to the Lazy S Ranch. Without a conscious decision and before the Mustang had shown in my rear-view, I was spinning the wheel and was headed down what was little more than a narrow and bumpy track.

I didn't kid myself, though. I hadn't shaken the opposition, because the cloud of dust I had left hanging was as good a marker as any they could hope for. But at least they were going to have to eat my dust.

In a few seconds, the Mustang was right behind me, to be seen fleetingly and eerily in the vast billowing cloud of particles in which we were travelling. Worse than the predatory throb of its motor, I three times heard the flat, dry crack of a gun, but there was no corresponding sound of a slug finding its mark.

The guy throwing lead couldn't hope to draw a bead with all that dust and the two cars bucking like stallions with burrs under their saddles.

The driver had a better idea. He gave up trying to overtake, only to be frustrated either by my driving or the narrowness of the road, and began to smack the rear of the Olds with the front of the Mustang. The second impact was so fierce that it jerked my head painfully. If he couldn't force me off the road, he was going to snap my head off at the neck.

Just then, I spotted that the track ahead broadened out. My pursuers would realize it too. They would try either to pass me or force me off. I wasn't sure I was a good enough driver or that my heap was responsive enough to stop them.

End of the line, Dev, I told myself.

Gritting my teeth, I yanked my seat-belt a shade tighter. Then I hit the brakes hard, at the same time pulling the wheel to the right. As I had calculated, the Olds swung around almost on its own axis and ended up facing roughly in the direction from which it had come.

The noise was deafening, the sensation sickening and disorientating.

Only afterwards did I work out what happened. As I pulled right and went into a slithering arc, the driver of the Mustang, to avoid a collision, pulled left—at which point his luck ran out. The offside front wheel hit a large rock, the driver lost control and the car rolled over and came to rest on its roof.

In my rearview, I caught a blurred impression of the inebriated tango.

When I cut my motor and climbed out of the Olds, coughing and choking in the swirling dust, I witnessed the last stage of the process—the Mustang settling down in a stricken clamour of groaning metal and shattering glass.

But that wasn't all. A door was kicked open, and a lanky negro, not visibly the worse for wear and tear, jacknifed out of the wreckage into an upright position. His teeth flashed wickedly, and there was a big gun in his fist—a .45.

While I was still recovering from shock, he squeezed off a shot, and I heard the bullet ripping through the foliage of some parched and stunted trees behind me. I ducked down by the hood of the Olds, yanking out my own piece. When I raised my head, the negro fired again and missed, but he was probably groggy, acting out of professional instincts of survival rather than with a considered plan, because when I half recoiled, he didn't move, as if waiting for the confirmation of mentally rehearsed triumph, and I checked my instinctive withdrawal, pointed my .38 at him and drilled him through the right shoulder as neatly as if I had taken careful aim.

'You mother!' he sobbed, but he didn't drop the gun, and that worried me.

It needn't have.

He threw one more slug, completely wild but to give me something to think about, before he took off, running shakily, and disappeared into long weeds and dwarf-clumps of trees.

I thought of following him until I realized with my first step that my knees were wobbly and the rest of me like a dipso's hand after a thirsty night. He was welcome to go—over that terrain, in that heat and carrying a .38 calibre hole in his shoulder.

Wiping the sweat off my face, I checked an inclination to throw up. I was drenched. I needed a towel, not a handkerchief. Then I walked towards the Mustang, my gun levelled in case of any more unpleasant surprises. My nostrils were flaring, ready for the sweet reek of dangerously spilled gasoline. I detected only the normal smell of a car that had been driven hard. The tank was intact, and there were no ruptured fuel-lines, with their tell-tale trickles of liquid.

One man was left in the car—the driver. Where the wheel had caught him, his chest was caved in, and he dangled grotesquely, held by trapped legs. He was a chunky little guy, bald and with a faintly surprised look on coarse, tired features. He had a right to it. I could tell at a glance he was dead, but I felt for a pulse in his limp wrist and was unsuccessful.

Unless I was going to hunt the fleeing negro, there was nothing else to do there. I didn't, right then, feel like searching the body for identification. Even if the man carried any, he was, I had a strong hunch, merely a hired pro.

The man I wanted was the guy who had paid him.

I got back into the Olds, started up and backed around the wrecked Mustang before I turned the car about and headed for the Lazy S Ranch.

After another mile down the undulating dirt road, I found it—or what was left of it. The Lazy S had finally become so lazy that it had flopped over and died. The air of abandonment was total, and I was surprised to find an inhabitant among the leaning bunkhouse, empty ranch-house and burnt-out barn. But there was one—a baked lizard of a man, around sixty, in tattered straw hat and denims that rivalled the buildings for decrepitude. He was living in what had probably once been the ranch's guest-house—now dark, untidy and evil-smelling.

I told the man there had been an accident and someone had been killed.

'That a fact?' he said, with as much response as if I
had brought tidings that flying saucers had landed.

'Yeah,' I said heavily.

'Don't get many of those.'

I asked myself whether he meant accidents, deaths or
something else. But he was the marooned mariner, I
figured, and I was the rescue-party. After so long alone
on the island, he was having trouble with his speech.

I asked after a telephone. To my surprise, he had one,
and I got in touch with the local sheriff's sub-station,
where a deputy who seemed glad of something to break
the monotony said he would be right out.

The old man was long on staring and short on words.
Rather than endure the unblinking gaze of those dark
eyes in their crinkled-parchment setting, I said I would
drive back to the wreck.

'Guess I'll come with you,' he said.

And he did—showing all the emotion of a Russian
diplomatic negotiator. Yet despite—or maybe because of
—his laconic response, I sensed this was the biggest news
since Gettysburg.

I wanted a belt of whiskey, but after we had reached
the point where the chase had ended, I began to feel as
though I'd had one—several stiff, mind-jolting belts.
The evidence of the senses was powerful, but when one
sense contradicted another, panic as well as bafflement
tended to set in, and I felt panic when I didn't see what

I expected to see, what I had remembered.

As though he'd known all along he was going to be disappointed, the old man looked reproachfully at me.

The Mustang and its dead occupant had completely disappeared.

Chapter Six

There were events you couldn't anticipate, and I had just witnessed one of them, but as I resumed my interrupted journey to LA, I had one bitter self-reproach to chew on: I should at least have made a mental note of the Mustang's licence-number.

Since several hours of daylight were left, I resolved to make good use of them. I tried calling Deborah Hartman, but there was no reply. I thought that I had probably—almost certainly—been tailed as I left her place, and I wanted to warn her.

Intentionally or involuntarily, she had undermined my faith in my client. Unless she was lying, he hadn't levelled with me about his relationship to Victor Hartman. I wondered what else he had suppressed, modified, embroidered or doctored in the hundred different ways up to and including a downright lie. I made up my mind, anyway, to check out Hartman's apartment, and the decision, though I chose not to analyze it, implied some sort of judgment of Samuel Bishop—at least a disinclination to take his information at face-value.

I guessed that Bishop had gained entry to Hartman's apartment, a cheerless little cell in a multi-storey block in Westwood Village, by flashing dough around. I tried something different—and considerably less legal. I tricked my way into the apartment-house by the simple and never-failing expedient of pushing the buttons over several mail-boxes and waiting for one of the occupants to trip the latch on the main door. The small foyer breathed antiseptic but characterless opulence. I took the self-service elevator to the third floor, where Hartman's pad was located. I tried the buzzer, but there was no reply. Four seconds later, I was inside the apartment—courtesy of the Bank of America. The lock would have disgraced a kid's moneybox, and the credit card slid lovingly between the jamb and the lock, which snapped back under carefully applied pressure.

The apartment was what I might have expected of a transient—a man who had finished a long-standing marriage but had not yet worked out his new life-style. The setting was functional, furnished largely by scores of books, many of them standing around in stacks, without shelf-space. Even so, the apartment had the austere neatness of a disciplined bachelor. However, I hadn't come here to indulge in that sort of character-anaylsis, and pausing only to note the preponderance of scientific titles among the books, I checked the closets. Bishop hadn't lied: Hartman had moved out most of his clothes, and the garments left were mainly casual wear, the very items he might have been expected to take along had he been vacationing. I inspected the small kitchen, which was tidy and unremarkable, devoid of signs of a hasty departure. The bedroom, predictably, presented the same opaque neatness. Even Hartman's desk yielded only anonymous evidence. Either he had carefully sifted the contents or he was not the sort of man to keep personal documents anywhere but in a safety-deposit box.

I was beginning to think the apartment was *too* impersonal, like a well-cleaned motel-room, when I spotted a book placed on a low table near a comfortable-looking chair. I picked the volume up—Leslie Fiedler's *Being Busted*. I had read it myself—an academic's scathing account of how he got stuck with a phoney narcotics-rap, the author introducing some shrewd asides about a whiskey-culture's moral aversion to drugs. I didn't know, though, whether the book furnished any fresh information about Victor Hartman, its presumed reader.

Probably not.

I was about to put it down when an empty matchfolder slipped from between its pages. I picked it up and studied the printing on its cover: Delgado's, Lankershim Boulevard. I dropped it into my pocket. Maybe it meant something, maybe not, but ever since a dying man had pressed one into my hand and helped me crack a case,[1] matchfolders had been quite a talisman with me. I hadn't, so far, cracked any more cases with one, but I continued to handle them with a gravity that I didn't

[1]*See* You'll Never Get to Heaven

61

normally bestow on such mundane objects.

It was about time I got lucky again.

I found out with ease where Mrs Yvonne Huffaker lived, a beautiful Spanish colonial house in a quiet street in Laurel Canyon. Her husband might have been rich, but either he didn't go in for that sort of thing or he had yet to graduate to one of those private estates with private police that sometimes made surveillance an impossibility in Los Angeles. I drove to the address, parked near the open twelve-foot wrought-iron gates at the foot of a short drive and sat there hoping that maybe Victor Hartman would show or—if that was too much to expect—that the lady herself might take off for a rendezvous with him.

There was a snag to the second contingency, though. I didn't know what Mrs Huffaker looked like or what make of car she drove.

Any more than I was sure that Deborah Hartman had given me a hot tip.

Most of two hours passed. A panel-truck made a delivery—flowers according to what I read on its side. Three or four cars visited other properties and left again. For a while, a guy in a Chrysler parked in back of me, looking at what could be seen of the houses—most of them set back from the road—like a real-estate fancier. Once, squinting in the rearview, I saw him produce a camera and poke it towards the Monterey cypresses on the opposite side of the road, but if he had planned on photographing one of the spreads, he must have thought better of it, probably concluding the view was too obscured by luxuriant foliage, because he put the camera away without, so far as I could tell, making the shot, and shortly afterwards drove off. He wasn't a cop, I decided, and he took no interest in me. On the other hand, if he was a PI, he had behaved in a screwy manner that made no sense to me. I forgot about him, my interest briefly stirred by a passing Rolls with a hard, lacquered doll at the wheel. After its disappearance, the neighbourhood once more subsided into affluent seclusion and indolence.

My nerves were mending—not without aid. I nursed the quart of bourbon I had bought once I shook free of the incredulous sheriff. From time to time, I took a pull, imbibing enough to get mellow without getting sloppy; and as I swallowed, I thought about the afternoon's events and the disappearing Mustang.

It took quite a measure of booze to induce even a modicum of mellowness.

Dusk was thickening and I was thinking of calling it a day when a white Aston Martin nosed its way along the drive I was watching and made a right turn as it cleared the gates. I wasn't sure who was at the wheel, but it was Victor Hartman's car, all right.

My luck began and ended right there.

As I tossed the quart on to the rear seat and leaned forward to start up the Olds, someone yanked open the door on my side.

'Hey, bud,' he said, 'this is private property. What you doing?'

In the heat of the moment, I considered taking off anyway, but from the way he was holding on to the door, I had an idea I would end up dragging him with me. Aided by the gathering shadows, he had crept up on me unobserved. And if he had come unobserved, I reflected, he had done so deliberately.

He was as tall as I was, about six-three, but considerably broader. If you looked closely, his coarse, tanned features carried subtle traces of pugilism—nothing overt like a broken nose or pounded ears, but the tiny signs such as a mere suggestion of scar-tissue that some employers found attractive in a handyman, a chauffeur or even a butler. If he was any of these, however, he wasn't in uniform. He wore a loose-fitting dark suit, and the sunny smile that contrasted with it announced total confidence and dismaying insensitivity to the discomfort of others.

Like mine, for instance.

Impotently, I watched the Aston Martin disappear into the gloom.

I winced and said, 'The houses may be private property, but if the street is, it's news to me.'

'Yeah, you could be right, Jack.' His voice purred insidiously, as though he could concede my logic without losing a point. 'The rich get greedy, I guess—always trying to grab more. Anyway, you didn't answer my question.'

'Is that so? Would you mind repeating it?'

He laughed. 'I asked what you were doing.'

'What's it to you?'

'I'm asking.'

'It's been a long, hot day,' I said, 'but I might just climb out there and reconstruct your looks. It might be worth working up a sweat.'

'Aw, you wouldn't do that, Jack. You ain't that tough or that mean.'

'Don't bet on it.'

He leaned forward slightly, unbuttoning his jacket so that I could just see the revolver he was carrying in a shoulder-rig.

I nodded. 'Local vigilantes, huh?'

'Now do I get an answer?'

'Why not? I resent the question, but I've nothing to hide. I'm doing nothing. Until you bust it up, I was sitting here and just thinking.'

'Thinking?'

'Why not? It's eccentric, but there's no law against it. Oh, and I was drinking, too. You can see the bottle for yourself on the back seat.'

He glanced at it with a sideways flick of his eyes that said he wasn't really going to take his gaze off me in case I pulled something fancy.

He demanded, 'What was you thinking about?'

'I need a violin to do this properly. I told you it had

been a long, hot day. My wife left me a note. She's run off with my best friend. I'm stuck with two kids to take care of. My best friend—can you imagine that?'

'They're usually the ones. Everyone's got problems, Jack.'

'Oh, you're a great philosopher. So what?'

'So take yours someplace else. We got our quota round here.'

'Nice neighbourhood,' I said. 'Real friendly.'

'Sure. We're bucking for the good citizenship award this year. No litter—especially no beat-up cars kicking around with beat-up losers in them—'

'Admiring the sunset and contemplating life's ironies,' I completed.

'Like you said, Jack. Now beat it before I get crude.'

I growled, 'If I didn't have to get back to those two poor motherless kids—'

'Sure.' He laughed, as unconvinced as I was unconvincing. 'Try me some other time.'

There was nothing else to be done. I had put on a show, perhaps one just crazy enough to convince him that I was a harmless nut or at any rate without interest in the recently departed Aston Martin. His coincidental arrival bugged me, though. Where he had come from and who had sent him were topics that interested me powerfully.

He closed the door, and I engaged drive. As the Olds pulled away, I looked back. Until I lost sight of him, he remained standing in the road.

When he finally turned and walked away, I was long gone, so that I could only guess that he disappeared into the drive leading up to the Huffaker house.

Chapter Seven

In the cruelly competitive world of LA, an area which had several nightspots where struggling aspirants actually performed for free, Delgado's was a useful showcase for young jazz musicians. They didn't perform for free, and most of them were established artists, but they were seldom big names, and Delgado's provided a setting in which music-buffs could hear them while at the same time professionals—agents, managers and impressarios —could scout for that year's Wunderkind, whom they were as likely to find at Delgado's as anywhere else.

Both performers and audience took their music seriously. The large room was not crammed with tables, because the management didn't hustle drinks in the manner of more conventional establishments. There was little talking during numbers, and if the waitresses served liquor, they took care not to rattle glasses.

I knew of no law against an electronics-genius being a jazz-aficionado, but what I had so far learned of Victor Hartman did not contribute towards a convincing picture

69

of him in that role. I hoped the match-folder wouldn't turn out to be a useless clue.

At the time I arrived, Delgado's had scarcely warmed up. A bass-player was uncovering his unwieldy instrument while a studious-looking pianist played tentative, exploratory arpeggios. But the serious stuff would probably not begin for at least another half-hour, and so far no more than twenty customers had shown up. I sat at a table in the shadows and ordered a whiskey sour from a diminutive blonde with features like a Barbie doll.

When she brought it, I asked casually whether she could assist me in a small matter.

As though she'd heard this line before, a wary expression settled on her features.

'That depends,' she said neutrally.

'Take it easy. All I want is information. There's a guy I'm looking for.' I shoved Hartman's picture at her. 'I know he comes here occasionally, but I don't know where he's living now. Ever seen him?'

The girl studied the photograph as if it might blow up in her face. 'He does seem kind of familiar. Yes, I guess he's been in here recently. But I really don't know who he is, sir, or where he lives.' She sized me up rapidly. 'Esme is in charge of the floor-service here. She might know. Shall I send her over?'

'Thanks. I'd appreciate that.'

Esme turned out to be as tall as the first girl had been tiny. Even so, she looked good in the uniform white blouse and mini-skirt of dramatic red. She was a brunette in her late twenties, civil, but with a faintly imperious aura that said she was used to giving orders.

I repeated my spiel with Hartman's picture.

She smiled politely and asked, 'Fuzz?'

'Private, honey. And there's dough in it for you.' I added superfluously, since I had already seen the answer in her eyes, 'If you know him, that is.'

'What's he done?'

'Nothing—absolutely nothing. Somebody is worried about him, wants to know where he is.'

'Wife, huh?'

Deciding to let her think so, I nodded. The free-masonry of women made it a good bet that Esme would respond favourably to the notion of a deserted wife.

She said, 'He's been in here pretty frequently.'

'Starting when?'

'Oh, I don't know—maybe three or four months back.' She returned the picture. 'Yes, that's Mr Harkness, all right.'

'You're sure about that?'

'Positive. In a square way, he's kind of goodlooking.'

I decided she was too intelligent to have fumbled the name.

Harkness—Hartman. They were both two-syllable names, similar enough so that their user would remember the alias with ease, dissimilar enough for him to keep them distinct in a brilliant mind. Besides, the initial letters would expediently tie off loose ends such as monograms on baggage or handkerchiefs.

I said, 'Does he ever come here with a woman?'

She shook her head. 'No, I think I would have remembered. Several times, though, he was here with a man—a guy called Broderick. I remember the name from one time when there was a telephone-call for him.'

'Who made the call?'

'Well, I didn't take it, but I would guess it was Harkness because the message was that Mr Harkness couldn't make it. This was maybe two weeks ago. Broderick is a big tipper—the kind of customer you remember. I remember the both of them for another reason, though.'

'Which is?'

'They never arrive here together or leave at the same time. Delgado's is a sort of rendezvous for them. Nothing sinister about that, I guess.'

'No, I guess not,' I hastened to agree. 'What do you know about this guy Broderick?'

'Nothing—he's just a customer. I could give you a description if you like—tall, lean, dark, early forties, good manners, speaks with a slight accent, and, if I had to guess, I'd say he may have some Mexican blood. Probably a salesman.'

'What makes you say that?'

'I don't know really. It's just that sometimes I get the idea he's trying to hustle the other man. The conversation gets pretty serious—not an argument, I'd say, but like Broderick is trying to persuade Harkness.'

'Have you ever heard any of the precise words they use?'

She smiled. 'Mister, you don't know much about this game, do you?'

'How's that?'

'You can divide customers into two groups. There are those who don't give a damn what they say in front of you, because to them you're just part of the furniture. Drunken women mostly—you'd be surprised the stuff we hear. And there are the discreet, careful ones who change the subject or drop what they're saying the moment you get to their elbow.'

'And Broderick and Harkness belong in the second group?'

'You've got it.'

'So you don't recall any words?'

'Well,—' She frowned. 'Maybe one night I heard something. But it wasn't—you know, important.'

'Perhaps not. But try to remember the words.'

The frown intensified as she re-ran some private movie in her mind. 'It was Broderick. He said—this is just approximate, you know. He said: "The bus won't wait for ever. You could find out tomorrow you've already missed it." I mean, I could have screwed up the words. But that was what it came down to—something like that.' I didn't know what my face was showing, but she added with slight resentment, 'I told you it wasn't important.'

'Don't worry. You did fine.' I took out my billfold, slipped her some money and wrote my number on a card. 'The next time either of those men walks in here, I'd appreciate your calling me at that number.'

She licked her lips, professional caution not entirely dispelled by the dough. 'Look, I have to ask—is this on the level?'

'Yes. It's entirely legal, and you won't get into trouble. There isn't a house-rule against giving out information about customers, is there?'

'Not that I know of.'

'Well, then ... And what you've told me is scarcely indiscreet, is it?'

'I guess not.'

I gave her my best smile, which took quite an effort after the day I'd had.

As I left, the pianist went into a slow-tempo version of 'Happy Days Are Here Again'. Feeling better than I had since I left the apartment that morning, I thought that he just could be right.

Chapter Eight

'You're not happy about this case, are you?' Kay said.

'Even for an urbane, economical writer,' I replied, 'that must be the understatement of the year.'

All the usual palliatives and healing unguents, including her own soothing presence, were failing to work, it seemed. The water of the shower hadn't washed away my preoccupations, any more than Kay's cunning fingers had massaged them out of existence. In an old terry robe, I stretched out, trying to relax. It didn't work—not even with the aid of some quiet, superbly unemphatic jazz by Dave Grusin on the hi-fi. Alcohol, too, failed. The problems of my work were with me like ghosts, beyond exorcism.

Even talk hadn't helped.

'Let's go over it again.' Kay suggested, turning down the hifi. 'Mind if I make notes?'

'Mind? Hell, no! Be my guest. I'd welcome the perspective of seeing it all written down stone-cold sober —as I am, regrettably.'

'You shall have it.' She wasn't exactly overdressed. In

fact, a couple of layers of diaphanous nylon were all that covered her, so that, with a notebook in her hand and pencil poised, she looked like Playboy's idea of a very private secretary. 'What's bothering you?'

'To start with, my client, Mr Samuel Bishop. His aura of mystery turns me off.'

'Has he asked you to do anything illegal? Or even irregular?'

'I wish it were that simple. But he didn't level with me, and it wasn't out of shrinking delicacy of feeling. He lied about his relationship to Victor Hartman.'

'Or Deborah Hartman lied to you.'

'Why should she? It doesn't make sense.' I sighed. 'Anyway, what the hell is all that compared with what happened this afternoon?'

'If those men tailed you from Ventura, why should they be watching Hartman's ex-wife?'

'Good question, princess. It kind of pales to insignificance, though, if you think about the disappearance of that Mustang. There's one sheriff and his deputy who think that Brock Devlin will shortly be a candidate for the funny farm.'

'How far does their credulity stretch?'

'Oh, they were generous enough. With the tyre-tracks as corroboration, they believed my story of the chase. What they didn't believe was the climax to it. I can't honestly say I blame them.'

'Well, I'll play devil's advocate. You say the Mustang rolled over?'

'Absolutely. How does anybody make a mistake about a thing like that?'

It's not likely, I agree. But perhaps you made a mistake about the driver. Perhaps he wasn't dead.'

'If not, sweetheart, he gave me the best dam' imitation I've ever come across.'

'Let's say he wasn't dead,' she continued blandly. 'The coloured man could have returned. Together, they could have rocked the car and restored it to an upright position, couldn't they? It is theoretically possible, isn't it?'

'Theoretically—yes. Just. If the driver was alive and more or less intact. But try convincing me. I was there. The driver was dead, and the negro was both scared and wounded. Even if, by some fluke I can't begin to imagine, the driver survived and recovered consciousness, the negro was not, it seemed to me, about to return. If a man's behaviour signifies anything, his impulses were exclusively towards flight. Furthermore, neither of them was in a condition to right that car—if it could be done by two men unassisted and if it was still in good running-order. Besides, if they did all that, they sure must have acted fast.' I laughed scornfully. 'The whole hypothesis is a damned sight too iffy.'

'For the sake of argument, have it your way. Then what happened to the Mustang? How did it disappear so completely and so fast?'

'It beats me. If someone had turned up with a tow-truck, he would probably have left traces—before or after removing the car. Somebody on one of the canyon roads might have seen him towing the wreck. But that car vanished into thin air.' I frowned. 'There's something I'm overlooking, though.'

'Like what?'

'That's the hell of it. I can't say. But there's something —I'm sure of it.'

'Brock, darling, in a trade where evidence is what counts, you're not precisely overburdened.'

'I know it. On the other hand, I've always rated hunches pretty highly.'

'Were those men trying to scare you—or worse?'

'I think they were trying to scare me.'

'Then they must have got carried away. They rammed your car, they fired at you—'

'Oh, they were playing hard. But I don't think they were playing for keeps, that's all.' An idea gnawed at me. 'I'd better try Deborah Hartman again.'

I reached for the telephone, dialled the number and let it ring. There was no reply.

While I could think up a dozen innocent explanations, I didn't like that.

I had just replaced the receiver when the telephone rang. I picked it up and a voice said, 'Samuel Bishop here, Devlin. How are things going?'

'I think they're shaping up, Mr Bishop. I caught a glimpse of Victor Hartman this evening, but I lost him.'

'You lost him?' The tone was coldly incredulous. 'How?'

'The details will keep. What's more important is that I

78

now have a line on him. He's seeing a Mrs Yvonne Huffaker.'

'A married woman?'

'She's not a widow.'

I gave him the address to sweeten him a little, and he asked, 'How did you get a lead so fast?'

'Deborah Hartman. You were right, Mr Bishop. She proved informative.'

'I thought she might. Do you know where Victor is living?'

'Not yet.'

'You say you saw him and lost him. Did Victor see you?'

He sounded eager. Most of the time he acted like a computer. But now he sounded eager.

'I don't think so,' I said. 'After all, why should he be looking for me?'

'You're right, Devlin. He shouldn't. What else have you learned?'

'Enough—from Deborah Hartman—to confirm your notion that Victor may be undergoing some sort of spiritual crisis. She was using past tenses, though. She hasn't seen him in weeks.'

'Well, at least he's safe and well. We know that.'

'That's far from true. I wish I could give you a more hopeful report, Mr Bishop, but I have to be honest. I saw Victor's car, and I presume he was at the wheel. It seems logical, given the circumstances. But I'm not one hundred per cent sure. I certainly couldn't make out

79

any details like the possible state of his health.'

'Very well.' He thought it over. 'I have confidence in you, Devlin. What next?'

'If that *was* Hartman, I should be able to trace him without too much delay. I expect to have positive information for you tomorrow or the day after.'

'That's good.'

'There is just one point, Mr Bishop. Two guys tailed me from Ventura this afternoon. They tried to kill me.'

'They what?'

'Well, maybe not. But they worked hard at throwing a scare into me.'

'Why should they do that?'

'I was hoping you might be able to tell me.'

'Well, I can't. A man like you, Devlin, must make enemies. Are you sure they were connected with what you're working on?'

'It seems logical, but I could be wrong.'

'I hope you are. I don't like the idea that Victor might be in that kind of trouble.'

To say nothing of me, I thought. Maybe my client believed that kind of occupational hazard was unremark-able or at least the sort of thing I could take in my stride.

'Is there any reason why Hartman *should* be in trouble?' I asked. 'Or Deborah Hartman?'

'Not that I know of. But keep me informed.'

'Right. You don't have to impress me with your pater-nal feelings.'

I could have imagined it, but I fancied there was a small pause before he said, 'Quite. Victor is considerably more than an associate to me.'

He might have taken the bait, but I was not to be allowed to hear him gulp it.

While he might still be off-balance, I asked quickly, 'Do you know a man called Broderick?'

'No, I don't.' A short pause, then: 'Listen, Devlin, you're not telling me everything—I detect suppression.'

'That's right. There is more, Mr Bishop, but it's not hard evidence, so don't press me for it.'

'I want results—'

'I know it. And I believe I'm close to them, but for now optimism will have to do.'

'All right.' He thought it over. 'Very well. In a way, I admire you.'

'I don't quite get that.'

'It's simple. A lesser man would not be so reluctant to provide information without being sure of his facts.'

'Well, that's what you're paying me for.'

He disconnected, and I stared at Kay for a moment before I murmured, 'He knew my number.'

She wrote something on her pad, frowned, then put it to one side.

'He's a rich, powerful man,' she said. 'You know that.'

'Nevertheless, it's interesting.'

'Intrusive, too. But don't see too much in it.'

I brooded upon the call and its implications.

Trying to scrawl the arabesque at the end of the chapter, Kay said, 'Well, I'll type up these notes tomorrow. Maybe you'll have some more thoughts by then.'

Stubbornly, I refused to switch off. She touched my arm, but I withdrew so nervously an onlooker might have mistaken the gesture for revulsion.

She stared at me for a long moment—a therapist with a difficult patient.

'When I was eighteen, I wanted to be the greatest novelist of my generation.'

She said it out of a silence, and her words insinuated themselves softly into my ears like music—wise, resigned, gently teasing.

But I was in no mood to be teased.

'What the hell's that supposed to mean?' I demanded. 'Besides, you *are* the greatest novelist of your generation.'

'That's a highly subjective point of view.'

'Hell!' I growled. 'It's all subjective. Only reviewers, academics and prigs think different.'

'Anyway, regardless of your generous opinion, I settled for less. I have a sense of literary identity, a modest stature, and that's what's important.'

'Oh, I get it. I let things bug me too much. I'm scared of failure. Correction—another foul-up like the last one.'

'You didn't foul up. In fact, you recovered brilliantly after a dirty trick.'

'Oh, yeah.'

As she stretched out languorously close to me in that black negligée that enhanced some mysteries but kept no secrets, only perversity kept me away from her. While she frowned affectionately at me, I gazed critically at her

82

lovely features, which had a deeper mystery than the tiny frown. They were too generous yet perfect, and you would have needed to invent a new geometry to explain why that face was not marred by its own fullness.

She didn't hide her need of me, but she made a good job of masking it in a civilized manner.

'It's been a long day,' she whispered. 'Come to bed.'

I knew it had been a long day, felt it in the marrow of my bones. Yet that wasn't what she meant. She was talking of missing me. I could see in her eyes some bearable and profound knowledge of me—bearable, but faintly sad, as it had to be when her dependence on me was greater than mine on her.

Not that it was my fault, or that there was anything to be done about it. Before Kay, I had spent too many years alone, perfecting the armour of self-sufficiency— an armour that might have been as crippling as it was protective.

Irony was her trade—or a part of it. She clothed her desires in understatement, paradox and the neat twists of words that at once heightened them and ridiculed them. I recalled what she had said when we met again after a long deliberate period apart: 'There are times when I don't think of you for weeks, days—sometimes even for a whole hour.'[1]

I kissed her lightly on the lips. 'You go ahead. I'll be there in a moment.'

'All right.'

[1] *See* A Knife-edged Thing

She got up in a flowing graceful movement, smiling at me as I gnawed at my problems, as reluctant to let them go as a dog obsessed with a bone.

In the doorway to the bedroom, she paused and murmured, 'Brock, darling.'

I raised my head to see her pull the ties on her negligée. The insubstantial nylon slid to her feet with less sound than a wistful sigh. Her skin was a dramatic white, her body long and voluptuous, the hips gloriously wide after the slender girth of her waist.

'A light chore for you,' she said. 'Pick that up when you come.'

Immediately, I jettisoned Victor Hartman, Samuel Bishop and their enigmas. Light chores had always appealed to me, and I would carry out this one with loving care.

84

Chapter Nine

In the morning, I tried calling Deborah Hartman again. There was still no answer.

After that, I spent an hour or so in straightforward research—the sort of fruitful labour, surprising to an outsider, that you could accomplish without ever leaving the office. MVD gave me the licence-number of Mrs Yvonne Huffaker's car, a late-model Lincoln, and from other sources, I built up a description of her—a smallish woman in her early forties who dressed with calculatedly effective casualness and had a habit of wearing wigs over her somewhat nondescript hair. In some ways, her husband was a more absorbing study. At fifty, he was into his third marriage, the previous two having ended in divorce on the grounds of mental cruelty.

Lawyers' fictions had never impressed me, particularly in Southern California, where divorce was the ultimate ritualistic charade, a three-ring circus over which the judge presided as clown-in-chief. However, one of my informants, a businessman like Charlie Huffaker, assured me that the man was a genuine psychopath, an anti-feminist who viewed his wives in terms of goods and chattels. All the more surprising, then, that he had five years earlier married Yvonne Sheraton Harmer, the oldest daughter of a talented but genteelly impoverished academic family, her father being a retired professor of semantics who had lectured at Stanford and later UCLA. The present Mrs Huffaker, who had previously been married to an army major, a professional soldier killed in Vietnam, was a gifted amateur pianist, a connoisseur of fine art and an earnest student of literature—'quite a bluestocking', in the words that were used to me, and a more than highly improbable partner for Charlie Huffaker.

He ran an import-export firm that he had built up from near-bankruptcy along with a reputation for being ruthless in business, the owner of an ungenial personality that had cost him more profitable deals than he had been able to clinch. The two ex-wives had told lurid tales of his inflated vanity and an immature sexual jealousy that had reacted to compliments from other men as duellists, in earlier centuries, had reacted to secret assignations and whiffs of adultery. In matrimony as in business, Huffaker liked to buy talent: his wives, like his junior executives, were assets, repositories of talents he himself lacked, and he resented any attempts, real or imaginary, to woo them away from him. He was I was told, an aggressive bantam of a man, whose one real fascination was his dynamic acquisitive impulse. He had, however, another and subtler, if not more sinister, quality: more than one had been deceived by a surface charm that implied some deliberate holding-back, a controlled biding of time, until the true man revealed himself.

My telephone-calls through, I leaned back in my chair and digested the information, some of it—as almost always—slightly contradictory, but with the main trends bold and unambiguous, the way I liked them to be.

If Victor Hartman was seeing Yvonne Huffaker, I didn't suppose they spent their time discussing the space-programme. For his part, Charlie Huffaker sounded like the sort of man you couldn't deceive for long. Hartman was free, Mrs Huffaker wasn't. Samuel Bishop opined that Hartman was undergoing a psychological crisis, and that sort of crisis could have been the result of wanting a commitment that Yvonne Huffaker was incapable of making.

The juxtapositions were stimulating.

My concern, however, was to trace Victor Hartman, and I figured it was about time to reel in the most obvious thread, advancing towards him as I did so.

Having made sure of the address, I stationed myself outside Charlie Huffaker's downtown office. A side-alley gave access to a parking-lot, but anyone entering or leaving it would be seen by me. At twelve-thirty, a Rolls ghosted up to the main entrance. I didn't need the powerful binoculars I had with me to see that driving it was the vigilante who had thwarted me in Laurel

Canyon the previous afternooon. On this occasion, though, he was wearing uniform. After five minutes Huffaker came out and climbed into the rear of the Rolls.

I tailed it to the Beverly Hills Hotel, where Huffaker went inside. His driver remained with the car. I speculated about how extensive the man's duties were, but for the time being, obviously, his orders, were to wait for his master.

I didn't underrate him as a watchdog, and the presumption that he would stay put was all I needed.

I took off for Laurel Canyon and the quiet street where I had seen Victor Hartman only to lose him immediately. This time, I parked farther away from Huffaker's driveway to continue my sticky, boring surveillance.

An hour passed during which I ate the hastily purchased hotdog that was all that stood between me and starvation. The Rolls did not make a re-appearance, but just as the hour was up, Mrs Huffaker's Lincoln left the driveway with the lady herself at the wheel. She headed for LA, and I was a mere couple of seconds behind her.

Except when it was controlled by traffic-patterns, her speed didn't vary by more than two miles per hour. She was a cautious driver, certainly one who gave no sign of awareness that she was being tailed. After turning east towards Beverly Hills, she made a left on to Doheny Drive, finally reaching her destination in Maple Drive, a quiet street between Doheny and Beverly, just north of Pico Boulevard.

When she got out of the car, I had my first clear sight of her—a slim woman with sad features and the slightly but elegantly emaciated look of an ageing ballerina. She walked further down the block, glanced around uneasily rather than furtively, and then disappeared into a building called the Rubidoux Apartments that made up in muted luxury what it lacked in more colourful qualities. An anonymous box, it was nonetheless impeccably maintained and fronted by a wedge of grass that had been so assiduously tended that it was reminiscent of an English croquet lawn. The worst of renegade dogs would have thought twice about defiling it.

I let a full five minutes elapse before I climbed out of the Olds and went to inspect the apartment-house. I was scarcely surprised to discover the name Harkness on a freshly typed card fitted into the slot above the mailbox for Apartment 3C.

I had found Victor Hartman.

I returned to the car. I had a book, but the afternoon passed on crutches, as time always did on these jobs. I observed the comings and goings of the neighbourhood, and twice I began to think I was not alone in keeping some sort of surveillance. Each time, however, the guys in parked cars of whom I was starting to get suspicious took off well before my conviction became absolute.

Yesterday's events must have left me jumpy.

My vigil didn't end when Mrs Huffaker left at just after five.

Ready, I thought cynically, to greet her husband

lovingly on his return from the office.

She looked happier than she had when she arrived, but I could have imagined that. As I had been detailed to find and watch Hartman, I felt no impulse to follow her, but I was prepared for Hartman's appearance now that their tryst was over.

I had made sure that if he left by car, I would spot him. The ramp from the basement-garage came up on Maple Drive. There was a back exit, but I couldn't be everywhere at once, and if he left the Rubidoux Apartments on foot, I had to gamble that he would emerge from the front.

He did that—twenty minutes later. He looked exactly like the two pictures in my possession—Bishop's and the second one I hadn't needed but which had served as a ruse to get rid temporarily of Deborah Hartman. Even so, the photographs hadn't prepared me for a greater resemblance to Jack Kennedy than the one I had detected. Save for a slight academic stoop, he seemed to be in good physical shape—lean but wiry. He looked preoccupied, though—maybe even worried. He was wearing a white terry shirt, tan slacks and loafers.

I didn't think he would be going far, and it turned out I was right. I followed him on the opposite side of the street while he walked a couple of blocks, bought a news-paper, hit a machine for a pack of cigarettes and then headed back. He didn't behave as though he expected to be tailed, and I felt sure he hadn't spotted me. He had simply stepped out to take the air.

Since I didn't suppose he and Yvonne Huffaker had been playing pinochle, I understood that impulse after an afternoon of making love.

He went back into the Rubidoux Apartments, and I, grateful for the chance to stretch my legs, returned to the Olds and the leaden monotony of my task.

It was to extend for another three hours before the light in Hartman's apartment, which was on the front, went out and, a couple of minutes afterwards, the white Aston Martin nosed its way up the ramp.

When he passed me headed in the opposite direction, I had already started up the motor. Cursing my luck as soon as I saw which way he turned, I waited until he was clear before I made a U-turn and hoped as I did so that the manoeuvre wouldn't attract his attention in the rearview.

He took Sunset and Laurel Canyon, so that at first I thought he might be headed for the Huffaker place. But as he kept going in the general direction of North Hollywood, I began to understand his route.

Victor Hartman was headed for Lankershim Boulevard and Delgado's.

Chapter Ten

The hour being considerably later, the crowd was much thicker than on my first visit. However, in terms of not being spotted, the throng suited me. I gave Hartman five minutes to make his entrance and then followed. I saw him sitting at a table at the back of the room, and he was wearing a dark blue suit whose formality seemed more appropriate to the man than the casual attire in which he had appeared earlier.

He was not alone. The swarthy man with him had to be Broderick.

I told the greeter that I was unaccompanied and that I would sit at the bar. Recognizing me, the girl Esme involuntarily turned her head towards where the two men were sitting. I smiled at her, nodded and held a finger to my lips—signs which, if she interpreted them correctly, would tell her I knew of the presence of Harkness and Broderick and had the situation under control.

It had been a long, dry afternoon, and I put down two

93

D

large bourbons in succession before I settled down to tease the third. The two musicians I had seen the previous night were now making music together with a drummer and a baritone sax. The sounds they created were eclectic, owing most to Brubeck and Mulligan, but they had a firm substratum of technique, and occasionally some original turn of phrase or arresting harmony would show through the derivative stuff. Dashing into 'You Make Me Feel So Young', they stood it on its head in a way to do it no good. I had the hunch they might learn better, though, especially the pianist.

Broderick and Victor Hartman had no such hunch. They were neither analysing the music nor listening to it. They talked earnestly and softly right through the number.

When it was over, Esme took some drinks across to them, and during the spattering of applause, Broderick flashed his teeth at her and said something jocular. Hartman acknowledged her service politely, but he lacked his companion's easy conviviality.

Observing that they seemed set for a while, I found a telephone-booth before the next number began and called Al Brody. That morning, I had warned my partner that I might need his help, especially if it turned out that Bishop wanted round-the-clock surveillance. It was a point that had not yet been made clear to me.

When Al came on the line, I told him where I was and what I was doing.

'I could use you,' I added.

'Is it urgent?'

'Not exactly. But I could use you. Why? This isn't your poker-night, is it? If it is, look at it this way. I'll be saving you some dough.'

'Very funny. No, it's not my poker-night. I have a tentative date, though.'

'You and your cheap broads.'

He laughed. 'Listen, don't knock it. Dolls with empty heads and big boobies make for a restful existence.'

'They're also interchangeable, constantly available and even more alluring after a night off. Break the date.'

'Okay.' He quit the fooling. 'What's the pitch, Dev?'

'When Broderick and Hartman alias Harkness leave here, they're going to split. I'd like to know more about Broderick. My idea is that you should stick with Hartman while I follow the other guy.'

'Isn't that a little outside what Bishop wanted you to do?'

'Yeah. That misplaced initiative of mine—I'm stretching things again.' He was implying no serious criticism: each partner conducted his own case in the way he thought appropriate; and I had let him beef good-naturedly for long enough. 'Listen, are you coming or not?'

'I'll be with you in twenty minutes, Dev.'

'Make it fifteen. These two could take off any time.'

Al Brody was a big man with heavy-lidded eyes and a deceptively sleepy manner. His cultural aspirations ran to complaisant blondes, TV ball-games and twelve-year-old scotch. Over ten amicable and mildly lucrative years, I had found him to be fiercely intelligent and a dogged investigator, and if he had any pretensions, I had yet to encounter them. Al Brody was to the PI racket what Perry Como was to popular music—a superbly relaxed performer beneath whose somnolent veneer lay real talent backed by a wealth of experience.

He joined me at the bar, and without appearing even to glance at Broderick and Victor Hartman, he asked me to describe where they were sitting. He had seen them, though.

While we drank, he asked, 'What's your client's angle?'

'I'm not sure. I thought I was, but now I'm not. Do I have to be able to answer that one?'

'Not necessarily. But humour me. Make a stab at it.'

'Well, the angle is most probably a father's concern for his son. Not that I would care to analyse that concern too closely.'

'Why not?'

'Samuel Bishop is an egocentric guy—one who likes to think he knows what's best for other people. Furthermore, I suspect he's a moralist.'

'So?'

'Once he knows for sure that Hartman is zapping with Mrs Huffaker, he might apply pressure to break the thing up.'

'That bother you, Dev?'

'Not especially. He's paying for information, and I'm

supplying it. What he does with it is not my business.'

'Exactly.' My partner grinned goodnaturedly. 'I sure hope you mean that. It's a professional attitude.'

'Why shouldn't I mean it? I said it, didn't I?'

'You say a lot of things.' He drained his glass and nodded at the bartender for a refill. 'You're too sensitive for this racket.'

'You're always telling me that.'

'Hell, it's true!'

'There is truth in it,' I said uneasily. 'I'm pretty callous. If it wasn't there to start with, the years have put it there.'

'Yeah, but to me it comes natural. You have to work at it. There's the difference, Dev.'

'Oh, shove it,' I said rudely, because he was too accurate. 'Besides, it's showtime. The conference is over.'

I had the idea nothing was settled, though.

Broderick looked resigned and weary, perhaps even a little resentful. Victor Hartman seemed uncomfortable, as though he wondered whether he was doing the right thing or couldn't see the right thing to be done. Leaning close, Broderick made a final comment in what was presumably a low voice before he left the table.

'Here we go,' I said. 'I'm guessing that sooner or later Hartman will go back to Maple Drive. I'll look for you there. If it doesn't pan out that way, we'll wing it.'

'Like always, partner. When it comes to improvizing, we're the best.'

Since I didn't know the make of car Broderick was

driving, I left right behind him. I thought he hesitated a moment, like a man half expecting to be tailed, before he stepped out into the street, but I could have been wrong about that. Anyway, his pace picked up as he made his way to a late-model Ford, as anonymous as a rental car, which it might easily have been.

For once, my own heap was conveniently parked and facing in the right direction. When Broderick took off, the Olds was already rolling. The Ford headed south. Near Universal City, it stopped at a corner drug-store, into which Broderick disappeared for five minutes. I left the Olds, strolled past the front of the drugstore and saw him through the window making a telephone-call.

Perhaps I should have been suspicious about that, but I wasn't.

He returned to the Ford and resumed his journey, joining the Hollywood Freeway. When he left it, he turned east on Hollywood Boulevard. The size of the Ford's tail-lights never varied as Broderick kept up a steady lawful pace. If I'd had one, I would have trusted my maiden aunt to him as a passenger.

Eventually, he made a right and pulled up outside an unlit office-block next to a sporting-goods store. There was nothing other than proximity to connect him with either one of them.

So far.

Killing his lights, he climbed out and walked back in my direction. I kept low and waited, but he never made it as far as the Olds. He disappeared into an alley that ran between the two buildings. I climbed out and went to investigate.

It was just a narrow cement passage between structures, though there were doors on either side. I couldn't see Broderick, who might already have vanished through one of the doors. But, then, I couldn't see much. He could have gone right through the alley to where it came out on the other side. To have a hope of finding out, I would have to advance further into the darkness of the passage, and I didn't much fancy the idea.

As I was thinking it over, two men came walking briskly down the street, which was otherwise empty of people. They came without warning, as though they had been lurking in a doorway. When I became aware of them, they were already on me, moving a little apart so that I was between them.

Even so, I had time to pull my gun.

But I didn't—a mistake.

Instead, I tried to step aside. By stretching an arm out in front of me, one guy checked me. They both wore hats, and in what little light there was, I could not see much of their faces. The two were well built, though, and while I was registering the fact, the second guy took his right hand out of his pocket and flourished it in my face in a way that made the nickel-plated knuckles on it gleam dully.

'That takes care of the introductions,' he said.

'Not quite,' I corrected him as I smacked both hands into his body, feeling satisfied when he grunted hard and the flesh folded softly around my fists before he doubled up.

While I was congratulating myself, his partner landed a right to my jaw that rattled it with sufficient impact to throw me back half a dozen steps into the alley. In three gliding strides, he came after me and tried to swarm all over me, but despite feeling groggy, I managed to keep my feet under me, and I stopped the flurry of punches with two fast pokes just above his belt-buckle. After that, the evening air wasn't quite so full of fists, and when he again hit me with his right, I smiled grimly because the zip had already gone out of it and I knew that I could take him.

Before that stage was reached, however, the guy with the brass knucks was on the move again. I smothered his partner's left arm with my right, hung on to it, took minimal punishment from his right and caught the returning brawler with my own left, keeping it low to reach him where I had already twice planted mean blows.

The stunt came off.

Brass-knucks screamed as he rode a third low punch, and his partner got so confused that he paused. Pirouetting clumsily, I swung him against the wall before I broke free of him, at the same time planting a kick in the masculinity of the other man. They both floundered like newly landed fish. Considerably taller than either of them, I grabbed them by the napes of their necks, shook them till their hats fell off and then smacked the bare skulls together with a sound like someone racking up an impressive score in a pool-hall. After that, they were rag-dolls, and I let them flop on the floor of the alley while I caught my breath.

Still gasping for air, I crouched down by the slumped bodies.

Before I could reach for the first man's wallet, a voice said, 'Freeze, you lucky bastard.'

I thought it might be Broderick, but it wasn't.

Although I didn't get up, I didn't keep entirely still, either, and as I glanced up, I saw that a much taller man than Broderick or the other two had entered the alley from the street. He pointed a .45 at me. I could see that much, and that was all I needed to see, even if I did have a hankering for a clear look at the guy in back of it.

His words rankled, nevertheless.

'You can forget the luck,' I growled. 'These apes were outclassed by a gutter-fighter from way back.'

'I still say you were lucky.'

'Don't waste it on me, friend. When they come round, comfort the losers with your opinion.'

'Cocky, aren't you?' His voice was thoughtful, deliberate. 'Stand up slowly and stop thinking I'm your friend.'

'I never did,' I confessed as I obeyed.

He came closer to me, but I could still barely make out his features.

'That's good,' he said. 'You're tough, Devlin, but you're not that tough.'

His right arm described a wide horizontal arc, and the

101

revolver at the end of that arm slammed against the side of my head like the iron gate of eternity. With the same terminal ponderousness, I tumbled end over end into the abyss of unconsciousness.

Chapter Eleven

When I recovered, I still lay in the alley—a realization that surprised me slightly. I felt much more surprised, though, to discover that I had all my teeth and that my ribs weren't cracked—not to mention other more vulnerable parts of my anatomy. Retaliation evidently hadn't been part of the men's permitted behaviour. It looked as though their orders had been quite simply to stop me.

They had gone, of course. So had Broderick's car, though I didn't find that out until later—roughly, the eight or ten minutes it took me to get back on my feet without fainting or throwing up.

Then, shakily, I drove to relieve Al, stopping off at the office on the way to patch myself up with a cold compress, two aspirin and a stiff belt of Four Roses—in reverse order of importance. Pat Hayward had left a message on my desk. The sheriff and his merry men still hadn't located yesterday's vanishing Mustang.

I drove to Maple Drive, where Al was sitting in his car. From inside, he signalled one brief stab from a pencil-flash to let me know that it was safe to approach. I climbed in.

'What happened?' I asked.

'Dullsville. Hartman left Delgado's ten minutes after you and the other guy. He drove straight here, and he hasn't budged since.'

'What about out here? Everything quiet?'

'Yeah, I'd say so. Everything's been real quiet.'

Although I couldn't see his face, I could hear what was in his voice.

'But what?' I asked. 'We've been together too long for you to start holding out on me now.'

'That's the damnedest part of it, Dev—there's nothing I can tell you. Just that I have a feeling about this one.'

'Maybe I know that feeling, Al. Such as?'

'Such as perhaps we're not the only ones keeping tabs on Hartman. Don't ask me to be specific. Except about one thing. A half-hour ago, two guys drew up in a Plymouth. They talked for maybe five minutes, and then they drove away. I say they talked, but, hell, I don't know *what* they were doing! Maybe they were watching me.'

'Could be. Look, we're pros, and we don't often make big mistakes. Yet the back of your neck is pricking, the same as mine. If Hartman is under surveillance by somebody else, how come we haven't rumbled the guys doing it?'

'I don't know. Unless we're slipping. Or unless the sort of stake-out we're discussing is the type only a nation-

wide agency with scores of operatives could organize.'
I must have been probing the side of my head, because
he asked, 'Anyway, what the heck's wrong with you?'

'I walked into trouble.'

I told him about it and he suggested, 'Guys hired by
Broderick?'

'At first, I thought so. The pattern pointed that way—
with Broderick stopping off as he did to make that call.
Now I'm not so sure. I'd say they wanted to keep me
away from Broderick, all right, maybe even to teach me a
lesson. The screwy feature is that the third guy didn't
intervene until he had to.'

'What do you mean—had to?'

'He must have watched the whole damn' thing—at
first with no intention of direct involvement. But when it
looked like I was about to find out who the two goons
were, he had to stop me.'

'You could be right. Though who would want to keep
you off Broderick's back?'

'Good question. Any ideas?'

Al snorted. 'If you don't know, I sure as hell don't.
Anyway, what do we do next?'

I decided to call Samuel Bishop and find out what he
wanted. In any case, I was overdue for giving him a full
report.

He answered so promptly that he might have been
sitting there with his hand hovering over the receiver.
Thinking sourly that at this particular time it was an
unfortunate colloquialism, I gave him a blow-by-blow

account, supplying names, addresses and times. He sounded interested but about as emotional as Robert Mitchum in one of his early tough-guy roles.

He asked, 'Who is this man Broderick?'

'As I've told you, I lost him, so for the time being his identity is going to stay a mystery.'

'And yet he and Victor are meeting repeatedly. Devlin, do you think there's any chance this man is blackmailing Victor?'

'I've considered the possibility, but I'm not sure.'

'Someone who knows about him and Mrs Huffaker—'

'I follow the line of thought, Mr Bishop, though it would seem more logical for a blackmailer to put the squeeze on Yvonne Huffaker than on Hartman. Furthermore, that theory is far from comprehensive. For example, it doesn't explain the two attacks on me or Hartman's reasons for changing his apartment and his name.'

'At least you've found Victor, Devlin. That's the main thing.'

'Sure. Are you going to see him?'

'I think not—for the time being. Is he aware of your surveillance?'

'I'd say he certainly wasn't. But now it may be up to Broderick. If he knew he was being tailed tonight, he could tip Hartman off.'

'I believe we'll take that risk. Carry on with what you're doing.'

'Okay. Do you want this simply by day or round the clock?'

106

When he said the second, I groaned to myself—despite the thought of the extra money. Even if I had been in better shape, a round-the-clock stakeout on a two-man basis—one in, one out—was tough sledding. To make life easy, it should be a three-man operation.

While I was thinking it over, Bishop added, 'There is one other thing, Devlin. I'd appreciate a report in writing as soon as possible. If you like, you can send it to Acme.'

'Yeah. Which do you want first—the report or a tight watch on Hartman for the rest of the night?'

'You're a testy character, aren't you? I'll put it down to your recent rough handling, though.'

That was big of him.

He disconnected, and I went to break the bad news to Al.

Chapter Twelve

We split up the watch to give me six hours' immediate rest and the chance next morning, if I needed it, to check on Deborah Hartman in Ventura. Her continued silence, though I hadn't mentioned it to my client, was worrying me. My partner's case-load was temporarily zero, and he told me to think positively—namely, in terms of the extra dough Bishop would have to shell out for the stakeout.

I drove back to the apartment and Kay. I was concerned for her reaction to my appearance, but not too much. Over the years, she had developed a certain resilience and fatalism in the face of the possibility that I might crawl home after a beating or worse. There were wives, not necessarily callous, who accepted the chance that their husbands might drop with a coronary after a hard day at the office; and the situations were roughly analogous. The events might not take place, but to reject the occupations that could cause them might also turn out to be a rejection of the men themselves.

Before she made that adjustment, Kay had once

walked out on me, but it would not happen again

She became slightly pale and tight-lipped when she realized I was somewhat the worse for wear. But she ran a tub of water for me, and while I soaked in it, she doctored the bump on the side of my head. Then she fed me, listened to what I had to say and became busy with the clipboard and pen again.

Once I was through talking, I asked, 'Well, what do you think?'

She left that little pause I loved—the one that indicated a mature, intelligent woman was about to speak, not some adolescent girl who would jump in with both feet. Then: 'I think the dramatis personae is getting congested—suspiciously congested. And I also think I'll type up these notes and file away at least four copies in different places.'

'I like the way you think.' I slid my hand between the slit of her robe and lest it rest on the warm, silken flesh of her thigh and the down above it. 'I'm feeling better already.'

'You can quit being tough.' She disengaged my hand gently. 'And you can quit being sexy. You're coming to bed, and you're going to let me nurse you in my arms like a baby. It's about the limit of my maternal instincts, so you may as well enjoy it.'

She woke me near seven—for once, I could have slept longer—and made breakfast for me. Then I returned to the Rubidoux Apartments, outside which Al Brody had passed an uneventful night.

'Not a goddamned thing happened,' he complained. 'I've been fighting sleep all night. When you think of how I *could* have spent that time . . .'

Taking over, I had a similar experience. I didn't catch sight of Victor Hartman, and nothing occurred in Maple Drive more dramatic than the confrontation of two dogs out for a morning walkie who decided that honour was satisfied after a couple of minatory growls and eye-rollings. As I fought against drowsiness, I did some eye-rolling myself, until Al, returning chipper and bushy-tailed around eleven o'clock, relieved my monotonous vigil and left me free to check on the former Mrs Victor Hartman.

Before I hit the Ventura Freeway, I tried her number twice more.

There was no reply.

I left the Olds near the open end of the one-block cul-de-sac in which Deborah Hartman was living. The neighbourhood was mercilessly bright with sunlight, and nothing and nobody were stirring as I strolled towards her bungalow. Stabbing the door-buzzer only tired my finger, and venetian blinds frustrated my attempts to see inside. Making sure I wasn't observed, I went around to the back, where I was about to examine the french window when I was distracted by a rustling in the hedge that separated the backyard from the next property.

Keeping low, I crept up to it and then straightened up until I could see over the top.

111

I found myself staring into the rheumy eyes of an old man who wore a navy beret and a loud check-shirt. He looked frail enough to be blown over by a light breeze, and his surprise contained embarrassment and fear.

I knew him from the time before Hindemith was a guy you bought in the supermarket: he was your old-fashioned neighbourhood-snoop and busybody.

'Hi, there,' I said affably.

He gulped and stammered, 'Hello. I saw you at the front. Kind of thought I might help.'

'Oh? In what way?'

'She's not in—Mrs Hartman, I mean. Guess she must be away.'

'Well, thanks for the information, but how would you know that?'

A natural loquacity overcame his minimal reticence and fast-departing fear. 'Because the police were here on Tuesday night. They checked out the whole area.'

'What for?'

I felt my guts tighten a little. Tuesday was the day I had first driven out to Ventura.

With a touch of self-importance, the old man said, 'I sent for them because I thought I heard gunshots—thought they came from here.' His face fell somewhat. 'Must have been mistaken, though. The police found nothing. They said I probably heard a car backfiring two or three times.' He added eagerly, 'They said I did right to call them, though. Must have been three or four cars here.'

'That many, huh?'

In a screwy fashion, what he said about the sounds interested me. Most people took gunshots for backfires; this old boy, the cops had suggested, mistook backfires for gunshots.

I asked, 'Did you see anybody on the property?'

'No, I guess not.'

'What makes you say Mrs Hartman is away?'

'The officers said she wasn't at home Tuesday night, and I haven't seen her since then.'

'Then you must be right—she's away. That's a pity.'

'You a friend of hers?'

'Yes—a friend.'

'If you'd care to leave a message with me, I'll see that she gets it.'

'Thanks, that won't be necessary.'

He was probably lonely—a not overly bright man in his seventies who had discovered that retirement wasn't all it was cracked up to be. Or maybe I was wrong; maybe he had always been the way he was—peeking over hedges or around curtains, his ear hanging out a yard. And yet the cops, the way he told it, had treated him at least civilly. Perhaps the department had a policy of Be Kind to Senior Citizens.

I stared at him dismissively until he withdrew—at which moment I found out that far from being tall, as I had at first presumed, he was actually standing on steps. He disappeared, mumbling some sort of farewell.

Rapidly, I checked the garage, which was unlocked

and empty. Then I returned to the french window. One minute's work with a thin-bladed penknife secured me access. Taking the risk that the old snoop might have spotted me, I slipped inside. If the cops were summoned and found me in the bungalow, any explanation was going to sound pretty lame.

Speedily but thoroughly, I checked the interior, more impressed by what I didn't find than by what I found. It reminded me of Victor Hartman's apartment all over again, but it was even more impersonal. All Deborah Hartman's clothes were missing, and I discovered no papers or other personal belongings. On the other hand, there was no sinister evidence—no bloodstains on the carpet, no overturned chair, no sign of forced or hasty departure, nothing to lend credence to the old man's story, which had already been discounted by the police.

Just a house full of stylish furniture.

The empty chests and drawers didn't make sense. Or did they? Deborah Hartman, if she wanted to do so, had had a clear day between my two visits to clear out.

But why? And wouldn't the old boy have observed her departure?

Well, even he couldn't be peeking all the time. He had to get some sleep occasionally, and she could have departed by night.

I went back to the livingroom where Deborah Hartman and I had talked about Victor. Everything was neat.

Almost too neat.

I was about to turn away when I noticed that a picture, a passable reproduction of Picasso's 'Violon au Café', was not quite symmetrically hung on the wall. Furthermore, there was something wrong about the picture.

I didn't remember it from my first visit.

When I moved the picture, I found the bullet-hole in the back of it. With my knife, I prised out the slug—a mashed-up .38—which was still in the wall.

It took me a minute or so of digging and probing—too long for somebody else, who, probably with several other tasks on his mind, had favoured another method. He had removed and discarded the picture through which the bullet had smashed to embed itself in the wall, and replaced it with a second one—no doubt taken from some other room.

He would have gotten away with it, too, if he'd only taken pains to hang it absolutely square.

As I was thinking that over, I heard a car pull up outside. My immediate thought was that the neighbourhood busybody might have called the police.

Dropping the squashed slug into my pocket, I left the same way I had entered. The catch on the window had been so simple to trick open that I was able to close up behind me with the certainty that there was no evidence of my illegal entry.

With swift strides, I moved silently across close-cropped grass, heading for the corner of the bungalow. Just as I reached it, I came face to face with two men—

one well dressed and with a dapper moustache, the other a middle-aged character who might have been a kindly judge.

Equally well, though cast against type, they could have been hired hoodlums.

Involuntarily, I yanked out my piece and pointed it at them.

'Who are you?' I demanded as they froze with shocked expressions that said this sort of thing didn't happen in broad daylight in Ventura.

The guy with the moustache recovered first. 'I am Howard Digby, a respected realtor in this district, and this is Mr Randolph, a client of mine,' he declared in brisk, no-nonsense tones. 'Who the hell are you?'

It had to be kosher. Nobody was that good an actor, and Randolph's shock could not have been simulated. 'The name is Devlin. I'm a private investigator from Los Angeles.' I put my gun away before Randolph could keel over, and flashed my buzzer for Digby to inspect. 'What are you doing here, Mr Digby?'

With a thin smile that had no humour in it, he answered, 'I might ask you the same question. This property is on my books, and I was about to show Mr Randolph over it.' There was every sign that he was trying to dominate the situation. 'Now what's this all about, Mr Devlin?'

'I'm looking for the present occupier. She's proving rather hard to reach.'

'Mrs Hartman? That's scarcely surprising. Mrs

Hartman has left this address. Hence Mr Randolph's interest in the property.'

'Kind of sudden, wasn't it? She was here on Tuesday, and she didn't give me the impression she would be moving out so soon.'

'Yes, it was sudden, though since the owner rents the house furnished, there was nothing particularly to detain Mrs Hartman, who was, I gather, in something of a hurry. She had to return East—a family matter, she told me.'

'When was this?'

'Yesterday.'

'You saw her?'

'No, I didn't. As a matter of fact, she called me from the airport. You see, having already left, she presented me with a fait accompli.'

'And you didn't like that?'

'Not at first. The regular procedure is to check over the property and contents with the tenant. However, I know Mrs Hartman, who is a charming woman, as you'll surely agree, and her references were impeccable. In any case, the rent has been paid in advance for the next three months, and she said that in the circumstances she would not expect the money to be refunded. Well, I'm a businessman, but neither I nor the owner are that greedy. I shall return a proportion of the sum, since this is a lovely property—' He glanced meaningfully at Randolph. '—that will no doubt soon find a new tenant.'

Ignoring the sales-pitch, I asked, 'Then you have Mrs Hartman's address back East?'

'Not yet. She said she would be in touch with me.' He had answered fluently and ungrudgingly enough, but his frowns were coming thick and fast, and I sensed that he might want to trade information. 'Look, do I have to answer all these questions?'

'No, you don't, Mr Digby, but thanks very much, just the same.'

I decided to cut and run before he got around to interrogating me about the nature of my business and why I had been jumpy enough to flash the heater.

As things stood, all he had was my name plus the fact that I worked out of LA. But even that was more than I cared to leave behind.

I nodded to Randolph and said, 'I'm sorry if I startled you, gentlemen.'

I hit Digby with what I hoped was a fair imitation of the smile of Errol Flynn, the handsomest rascal ever to come riding down the pike.

Then, before they could say another word, I was striding swiftly away from them. I made it back to the Olds without anybody calling my name or running after me.

What I had to digest was unpalatable, and I drove back to LA in no particular hurry, mulling it over.

Nobody shot at me. Nobody tried to force me off the road. Dullsville.

Chapter Thirteen

Before I relieved Al, I carried out one more small piece of research with predictably negative results. From my contact with MVD, I found out who owned the car Broderick had been driving. Not surprisingly, it turned out to be registered to a car-rental agency, who, when I approached them on the subject of its present driver, said they didn't give out that kind of information. I had encountered one of those blank walls that were thrown across my path every so often—not to be circumvented by bribery or subterfuge.

I shrugged off the dead-end, however. Broderick's address wasn't that important.

Al looked happy to see me. The big event of his morning had been when Victor Hartman emerged from the Rubidoux Apartments, walked two blocks, bought a newspaper and some groceries and then returned.

Before we parted, I asked Al whether he had any appointments.

'Yeah,' he said. 'With a double bourbon and a beer chaser.'

'You could do me a favour—some research. Check out Deborah Hartman for me. Try the newspapers, and if you can get it, a picture might be useful.'

'Okay, I'll see what I can come up with. You in a hurry?'

'You might say I'm late. But, yes—I'm in a hurry.'

Thirty minutes after he had gone, I recognized Yvonne Huffaker's Lincoln as it pulled up outside the Rubidoux Apartments. She got out, wearing black pants and a white cashmere sweater, and disappeared inside. Again, her looks, diminutive but with a suggestion of steel underneath, had reminded me of a ballerina.

I made a written note of her time of arrival and settled down to wait.

Five minutes later, my door was yanked open, and as, startled, I glanced up, I found myself staring at the interestingly flawed virile good looks of the Huffaker chauffeur. In his pocket, his right hand was thrust forward in the hint that it held a gun concealed there. He could have been bluffing, but I didn't think he was.

He grinned. 'Aw, hell, I took you by surprise, didn't I?'

'It's getting to be a habit,' I said wearily.

'Yeah. Either I'm damned good or you're pretty sloppy, Jack.'

'I used not to be, but I've run into too many cut-rate tough guys lately. Like you.'

'Don't be a sore loser, Jack. Or maybe you're trying to provoke me—yeah, that's it. Well, I don't provoke easy.' He made a slight but eloquent gesture. 'Get out of the car, and keep it soothing. Jerky movements play hell with my nerves.'

He backed off while I climbed out with a grace that was positively therapeutic. I saw his eyes dart glances along Maple Drive to make sure I was alone.

Then he prodded me and said, 'Start walking for the corner, and take it easy. This thing has a hair trigger, and I ain't afraid to use it.'

'No? I find that hard to believe.'

'Try me.'

I didn't think I would. The slim chance that I might be wrong was deadly.

I must have looked depressed.

'Don't feel so bad about it,' my captor said. 'This way, you get to drive a Rolls.'

He was right. As we rounded the corner, I caught sight of the Rolls parked against the kerb. He must have left it there and come up on me from behind.

And if he had left it there, he must have been tailing Yvonne Huffaker.

He motioned that I should get in, and once I had positioned myself behind the wheel and he had settled on the passenger's side, he took out his gun, covered me and relieved me of gun and wallet. Discovering my licence, he whistled softly but with no special air of surprise.

He said, 'It figures. A private peeper. Can you be bought off, peeper?'

'It's been tried.'

'Successfully?'

121

'Not so far.'

'Then you're in trouble, Devlin. That means you got to be *scared* off.'

'Thanks, anyway, for not calling me Jack.'

'Cut the comedy and get the car rolling. She'll drive herself if you don't interfere, but you give me a bumpy ride, friend, and one stiff jolt could make me blow you apart. Keep it in mind.'

I started up the Rolls, moved off and asked, 'Where to?'

'The Huffaker place. I believe you know the way.' He inspected me closely. 'You don't look scared.'

'I'm not—yet. Things will get better or they'll get worse.'

He laughed. 'Right. Somebody wants to talk to you.'

'That would be your boss—Huffaker.'

'You're a deductive sonofabitch, ain't you?'

'Your duties include shadowing his wife, do they?'

'Hey, you're a smash with the guesswork! Ease off, Devlin, and watch the road. You ain't going to pump me, pal, so you might as well give up. Besides, things should be the other way round. Who hired you?'

'You know better than to ask that.'

'Do I? It may take some knuckles, but you'll tell.'

Leaving me to think over the threat, he lapsed into silence. I joined him. He wasn't the sort of guy who could be tricked into giving information, and our relationship left no room for smalltalk.

When we reached the Huffaker house, we went in

through the front door, which wasn't locked. As we transferred from car to house, he never gave me a chance. If he hadn't done this sort of thing before, he was a natural at it.

But there would be a moment, I tried to tell myself. There always was.

He prodded me into a small library, leaving the door open. Leather bindings by the yard served as expensive wallpaper, and there was only one window—a small one, high up. The concealed lighting was soft, almost too soft to read by, but I imagined its intensity could be increased. There was no desk, but there were two comfortable-looking leather chairs and a low table, on which the chauffeur placed his gun.

As he straightened up, I hit him hard on the side of the jaw.

The blow had to be fast, and it had to catch him off guard, and so it wasn't scientific. He staggered, but when I dived for the gun, he came up with my own .38 and rammed it into my ribs.

'Back off,' he ordered. 'You had no call to do that.'

He looked hurt, not physically but inside.

I moved away, mad enough to snarl, 'If you'd put the guns aside, I could take you.'

'Maybe you could.' He massaged his jaw slowly. 'Maybe you could—you're a rugged one. But it would be messy, and it ain't necessary. Now sit down and keep your hands still. You're lucky I don't tap you on the head to steady you down. But don't tempt me.'

I had had my moment, and I blew it. There would not be another, I could tell.

I sat down while he covered me. For five minutes, we didn't speak, and then I heard a car pull up outside.

Grinning savagely, I remarked, 'So now I get to meet your master.'

Chapter Fourteen

I was wrong.

Still holding the gun on me, he eased over to the door and called, 'In here, please, Mrs Huffaker. It's important.'

After a pause, Yvonne Huffaker walked into the room, her pace slowing as she took in my presence and the guns. When she looked to the chauffeur for an explanation, her expression was tense.

He said, 'I found him in Maple Drive. He's the same guy I found outside here two days ago. His name is Brock Devlin, and he's a private dick.'

Mrs Huffaker's shoulders slumped, but as she turned to me, I read in her pretty eyes a kind of fatalistic resignation. She had known all along that this moment would finally arrive, and here it was.

As for me, I was doing some fast arithmetic. If the chauffeur hadn't been tailing Yvonne Huffaker for his master, then he had been doing so for her own protection.

It was an interesting development, one I had yet to understand fully.

125

Mrs Huffaker said, 'I suppose my husband hired you to follow me.'

'No, he didn't. I can see how it may look to you, but he didn't. I've never even met your husband.'

The chauffeur made an impatient gesture. 'He's lying.'

'I'm not sure that he is, George.' After a defenceless moment, Yvonne Huffaker's shoulders straightened again, and there was a brave tilt to her chin. 'After all it would be so pointless to deny it.'

'He'd do it, though,' George growled, clenching the fist that didn't hold the gun.

I sighed heavily. 'If it's any help and you'll take the trouble to believe what can easily be checked, I don't handle divorce-work. If I'm lying about that, it's an even more stupid lie than the first one George claims I told.'

'That makes sense,' Mrs Huffaker said slowly. 'Even so, you could be lying.'

'But I'm not.'

She looked me over and something about the way she did it told me she prided herself on a gift of reading faces. I prided myself on a gift for playing poker, but on this occasion I didn't try to keep my features inscrutable.

Then she said, 'I think I believe you. Who's paying you?'

'Rules of the trade—I can't answer that.'

'If it's not divorce-work, what is it?'

'Same rules.'

She thought out loud. 'Deborah Hartman—but that doesn't make one iota of sense, and besides you said that line of work is not for you.'

Impatiently, George moved closer. 'Let me go to work on him. I'll get the answers for you.'

'No, George.' She shook her head, smiling sadly as if at a favourite child, not yet old enough to understand. 'Even if you could succeed, I hate those methods. We—we can't do that.'

She was thinking hard, and I knew that it couldn't be long before she made the right connections.

After a pause, she asked George, 'How often have you seen this man?'

'Just the two times.'

'Did he follow me when I left the house this morning?'

'If he did, he sure played it cool. I didn't see him. I found him sitting in his car on Maple Drive. I recognized the car.'

'Once when Victor visited me, once when I called on him ...' For the first time really scared, she shot a stricken glance at me. Maybe it was always like that: people feared most for those about whom they cared most. 'It's not me you've been watching—it's Victor.'

I neither confirmed nor denied the theory. I simply kept my mouth shut, because that was what I was paid to do in a situation like this.

I didn't like it, though. Intuitively, I responded more to Yvonne Huffaker than I could ever have done to my client.

In a different, consciously controlled tone, she went on, 'I don't know what you're being paid, but I have a great deal of money—'

I shook my head. 'It doesn't work that way, Mrs

127

Huffaker. Call it professional ethics if you like. If I could be bought off, I wouldn't stay in business long.'

She took a deep breath. 'Then listen to me. I imagine a private investigator is a good listener.'

I spread my palms, indicating George's gun. 'You have a captive audience.'

'What kind of man are you?'

George interjected irritably, 'You're wasting your breath asking this schmuck that kind of question.'

We both ignored him as I replied, 'I like to think I'm honest. There are values I put ahead of the lousy buck. I try not to let people use me for vindictive purposes. Does that help you?'

'I think so.' She nodded slowly. 'That—and the knowledge that now George has brought you out into the open, your usefulness must be strictly limited. I can tell you already know that. It's my guess that you'll explain it to whoever hired you—if he can't see it, too. In any event, I'm going to ask you to leave Victor and me alone. You must be working for someone who is more interested in Victor than in me. I can't think why.' She perched on the arm of the vacant chair and gazed fiercely at me as though she were willing me to understand what she said next. She picked her words with a care no doubt inherited from her father, the semantics-professor, and remembering my research, I thought that her voice revealed a sense of light and shade that would enhance her gifts as a pianist. 'Five years ago, I made a doomed, disastrous marriage. I could spend the next hour analysing my

128

reasons and motives, but of course I shall spare us all that. However, I had lost my first husband, and I was lonely—powerful enough reasons for any woman to seek a new partner. My choice—if I went in for anything so rational and considered—was Charlie Huffaker. I knew his first two marriages had ended badly, and people told me of his reputation in business. But I didn't listen, probably because failed marriages are a commonplace and I imagined a man's business-conduct was separate from his private, personal self. I was wrong. If I sought an excuse, my best justification might lie in Charlie's charm.'

She made an eloquent gesture that led my glance to a silver-framed photograph of a man who had to be Charlie Huffaker. He was dark, like an amiable monkey, his smile of the type usually described as disarming. A second picture placed close to Huffaker's likeness was of a little boy whose age could not have been more than four.

Mrs Huffaker went on, 'The marriage turned sour as soon as I realized I was a possession—a thing to be manipulated. Even so, I worked at it. Odd, how intelligent people are reluctant to give up what others less complicated might clearly see as a lost cause. Then earlier this year, I met Victor Hartman. The impossible happened. Two mature, relatively experienced people fell extravagantly, lavishly and youthfully in love. There was nothing muted or subdued about it—it was almost a cliché in its eagerness.' She smiled sadly. 'On the one hand, I had my husband—a jealous, possessive psychopath. On the other, I had Victor—brilliant, sensitive, a man hungry to give and receive love.'

Unable to keep silent any longer, I asked, 'Why don't you leave your husband?'

This time, her smile was wise, indulgent of my simplicity. 'I saw you glance at the other picture, Mr Devlin. I neglected to tell you that Charlie and I have a child—a son whom I love dearly. If it came to a split, I have grave fears that Charlie, technically the innocent party, might get custody of the boy for whose sake I have endured this misalliance for so long. Charlie is vindictive enough to do almost anything. For instance, a part of George's duties is to spy on me.'

I glanced at him in amusement. 'What went wrong?'

'My husband failed to realize that loyalty can't always be purchased.'

George gazed at her with the sort of devotion on which dogs had all but cornered the market. I was beginning to understand a lot of things.

I commented, 'You're still not in a wringer, Mrs Huffaker. I know a lawyer—'

'There are other ingredients, 'she added.

'Such as?'

She pondered the wisdom of telling me more. Then: 'Victor is anxious to leave the country. The reasons are too complicated to explain to a stranger, but they have to do with his work, among other things. I'm not sure that I'm ready to join him in self-imposed exile.'

'And there's your son.'

'Yes—there's my son, too.'

130

'Is it so hard to reach a decision?'

'I didn't say that.'

She had almost made it, I could see, and I guessed what it would be.

I asked, 'Why all this self-revelation, Mrs Huffaker?'

'Isn't it obvious? I don't know for whom you're working, I don't know much about you, but I think there's a chance that you might see Victor and I deserve a stab at happiness.'

'Or my client might?'

'Yes—your client. I don't understand this. Is he a blackmailer?'

'I don't knowingly allow myself to be used by blackmailers.'

'If you know Victor, you know Acme Electronics, the president of which is as possessive in his way as my husband. If Sam Bishop thought—'

Whatever she had been about to say, she checked herself in time.

'Is that so?' I was back playing poker again. 'Mrs Huffaker, don't bother with the fishing expedition. The name of my client is confidential. Unless George can manage to beat it out of me. And it seems you're not about to let him do that.'

'Perhaps I should. In a cruel world.'

'No. It's not your style.'

'Your client—can he harm us?' she asked with more than a hint of desperation. 'I take it you've reported to him already.'

'I have. I suppose he could harm you. I suppose anyone might harm you by feeding information to your husband. My client's motives didn't seem so bad—questionable, maybe, but not bad.'

'You used a past tense there, Mr Devlin. Does that imply doubt?'

'I can't answer that.'

'After this—will your client have any further use for you?'

'It's not likely.'

Her relief was obvious. I was going easy on her, and I didn't want to go easy on her.

I said, 'There are other PI's though. Some of them could be smarter than me.'

She had dealt nobly with one threat. In an ignoble world, I showed her there were plenty more—ready to be purchased, eager to serve.

After a pause, she said, 'I may have told you too much. Or too little. In any case, I don't think continuing this conversation will serve any useful purpose.' She turned her head slightly. 'George, escort Mr Devlin off the property.'

There was more I wanted to say, but I was gagged not only by professional embarrassment but also by a thousand confused and confusing thoughts.

She might not have said too much, but she had surely said enough.

George prodded me with the gun, I got up and he walked me to the door, at which we paused when Mrs Huffaker said, 'George—no violence.'

'No—no violence.'

He didn't look at her, but his tone was gentler than I had heard it before.

He marched me down the drive, then put away his gun and returned my own to me.

'You're all bluff,' I said, 'and so is she—letting you wave that piece around like that.'

His voice thick with a barely checked sob—whether of rage at me or grief for his mistress, I couldn't tell—he said, 'Get out of here, Devlin. You can thank God for that lady. She's one in a million.'

He was right. Her principles had no place in the world we inhabited. That was what worried me.

'I know it,' I said. 'Take care of her, George.'

133

E*

Chapter Fifteen

By the time I recovered my car, I was hot and dusty. Continuing the stakeout seemed pointless, since there was a good chance that Yvonne Huffaker had been on the telephone to Hartman within seconds of my leaving her; and so I drove to the office.

A lot was on my mind. For example, Mrs Huffaker's fear: was she scared of Samuel Bishop, the man who, it had already been said, had dominated Victor Hartman's life; or did her fear have another source—some knowledge of her lover that was a secret to me and maybe to Bishop himself?

In the outer office, Sue Garner said, 'Al asked me to tell you he's sacking out at his apartment until he hears from you. He's left an envelope on your desk.'

I went in to inspect its contents. The first thing I saw was Al's note: 'Somebody played you for a sap, Dev. Deborah Hartman is in Hartford, Connecticut—where she has been living for the past eight months.'

The other item was a photocopy of a newspaper pic-

135

ture, the date showing that it was two years old—Mrs Victor Hartman, with husband, at the Music Center Pavilion. It was Hartman, all right, but the other face above the caption bore minimal resemblance to the features of the woman I had interviewed at Ventura.

My senses reeled from the impact of one shock too many.

'Jesus Christ,' I said softly to myself, the smell of a set-up rank within my nostrils.

The trouble with this business was that sooner or later you had to trust people, if only your client.

Samuel Bishop, who had steered me to the woman at Ventura, had to know of the impersonation.

Didn't he?

There was a way to find out.

I had already stalled too long calling him to relate the bad news that I had blown the surveillance. I dialled his number. Somebody who sounded like a butler and was unimpressed by my name said that Mr Bishop wasn't accepting any calls at present and hung up before I could react. My temper flaring, I dialled again. This time, all I got was a series of screwy noises. I took it up with the operator, and after a while I was told that the number was temporarily disconnected, whatever that meant.

I was mad, but I was more than mad. Anger was starting to run a bad second to curiosity.

Respectful of his secretiveness, I had not troubled to find out my client's address, but now I did so. It wasn't that I had forgotten Bishop's advice that if I came calling, I better have a damned good reason.

I had at least six damned good reasons.

Samuel Bishop owned a mansion just off Beverly Glen Boulevard in Bel Air, the kind of spread that vast materialistic assumptions had taught a whole continent to dream about. In different circumstances, I might have admired its architecture rather than its symbolic qualities, but there were two police black-and-whites with flashing red lights cluttering up the driveway.

The sight of them gave me a gut-feeling of the unpredictable, the incredible.

A policeman on the door stopped me, and I told him who I was and, lying a little, that I had an appointment with Bishop.

'What the hell's going on?' I demanded.

'Say, maybe I know you. Weren't you on that boat that blew up at San Pedro?'[1]

'That was me. And I'd still like to know what's happening.'

Losing interest in me, the cop said, 'You'd better take that up with Lieutenant Martinelli. He's inside.'

I encountered him in the entrance-hall, which was no bigger than the average public library. The lieutenant was a short, dark, irritable man in his late forties who looked as though he would like to make captain before he retired and didn't stand a chance.

When he heard my trade, he showed a flicker of

[1] *See* You'll Never Get To Heaven

interest, demanding, 'What's your business with Bishop?'

Everybody was asking the forbidden question that day.

'You know better than that, Lieutenant. Private, remember?'

'Not any more, it isn't. At approximately 3.30 this afternoon, Bishop took a Colt .45 automatic from a drawer in his study, inserted the muzzle in his mouth and squeezed the trigger. Messy, but very final. Now about that private business—'

I said automatically, 'Bishop hired me to check into the whereabouts of one of his people in Acme Electronics. He had a fatherly interest in the man—a certain Victor Hartman.'

'I see. Well, nothing there for me. Or for you any more.'

'You're saying this was suicide?'

'No question about it. There was no note, but time was running out for this guy. I don't know how much you know about him, but he'd already had most of his stomach removed—cancer. He was in constant pain, sometimes severe pain.'

'Who found the body?'

'Fredericks, a manservant. Bishop, normally an early riser, got up late and complained of feeling very ill. Fredericks wanted to call the doctor, but his boss wouldn't let him. Bishop refused lunch. At 3.30, Fredericks heard a shot in the study. When he went in there, Bishop was slumped over the desk.'

'Mind if I look at the body, Lieutenant?'

'I don't see the point, and it's going to turn you over. But if that's the way you get your kicks, be my guest.'

He showed me into the study. A sheet covered the body, and at a sign from Martinelli, a uniformed cop drew it aside. I avoided looking at what had been the head. Bishop had been wearing a red velvet smoking-jacket and dark trousers. But it was his hands that drew my attention.

They were wearing no rings, and the nails had been cut extremely short.

For a moment, I was back in the black Mercedes. I heard again those prophetic words from my client: 'Pain and I are old friends—old enemies, at least. Pain you don't come to terms with, though you may cheat it at the expense of life itself.' The man who said those words was wearing austerely expensive rings on immaculately manicured hands.

I jerked myself back to the present.

To be sure, I took a closer look at the body. There were no rings and no signs of any. If a habitual wearer temporarily left them off, the impressions always showed. Furthermore, the nails hadn't been recently clipped, either. The dead man had been in the habit of wearing them unusually short.

Without photographs or without interrogating the manservant Fredericks, I couldn't be absolutely sure, but I was looking at Samuel Bishop, I had no doubt.

Yet the man who had interviewed me in the black Mercedes had not been Bishop.

Another impersonator. Another diligent, painstaking and perhaps even brilliant impersonator.

But not Bishop.

Maybe my complexion registered inner turmoil, because Martinelli said, 'Take it easy, Devlin.' He nodded again to the cop, who replaced the sheet, and asked as he walked me to the front door, 'How well did you know Bishop?'

'Not well. I met him only once.'

'What was your impression?'

'He was a bundle of laughs, but in this racket, Lieutenant, you don't work for them just because you like them.'

'Yeah, I know the problem.' He nodded gloomily. 'Tough old bird, they tell me, like you said. The sort of guy who would want to face death on his own terms.'

'Why not? He'd been dominating situations and people all his life.'

'You say he hired you to check on a Victor Hartman?'

I could tell that the question was purely routine. Martinelli had no interest at all in Hartman, but I gave the lieutenant his address.

After that, I left. But not immediately.

The doors of the four-car garage were open, and without being obvious about it, I managed to look inside. A black Mercedes was there, all right, and it was the same one in which I had ridden with the fake Samuel Bishop.

Chapter Sixteen

The abortive nature of the whole case would not let me dismiss it as a bad dream.

I had written things off before—loose ends, bizarre coincidences, unexplained events, sometimes even whole investigations. But this one was different—and not merely in magnitude. I had more than a professional hatred for so many mysteries, but another ingredient offended me even more : I had the acute sensation of being manipulated and deceived, and I didn't like it at all.

As a sort of standard operational procedure, I should have obtained authentic pictures of Samuel Bishop at that point, but knowing what they would prove, I rejected the idea as wasted effort. I went back to the office, sat at my desk and thought. Brooding over untidy cases —and almost all of them were, to some degree—was a weakness of mine. This one, though, yielded no logic, no pattern, no form—merely the arbitrary and the grotesque.

Like two bars of music lurking in the mind, beyond

exorcism, Kay's phrase about too many dramatis personae haunted me.

Eventually, I called her, told her to be ready with her clipboard and gave her a detailed but concise account of the day's events. She made few comments but asked all the right questions—not the obvious ones, but those that would stimulate fresh thought, subtly angle for a different perspective from my own, which was proving so sterile.

She knew me too well and asked, 'How long do you aim to sit at your desk with only the office-bottle for company.'

'I'd forgotten about the office-bottle, but thanks for the suggestion. The answer to your question is for a while longer. Right now, I wouldn't be very good company.'

'You wouldn't have to be, darling. I don't stay with you for your sunny disposition, you know. Take all the time you want, but don't get too blue.'

'I'm not blue exactly—'

'You can't win 'em all.'

'It's not winning I'm worried about. My batting-average is getting lousy, though. What are you going to do?'

'Type up these notes, I guess.'

'Good girl. And, princess, get rid of the copies as you said you would. Don't even tell me where or with whom. I'd like to think of them stashed away somewhere other than the apartment.'

'It shall be done. Fears aren't always specific, I guess, but you have something in mind?'

142

'No. Let's say my cautious instincts are working overtime.'

After I had disconnected, I pulled open the bottom drawer of the filing-cabinet and poured myself a therapeutic shot of Four Roses. Five or six on the same scale would have helped me work up a little professional optimism and a modicum of philanthropy, but I didn't intend to get that well oiled.

If I had, however, what happened ten minutes later would have sobered me up fast.

Sue came in, and I thought, until I looked at her face, that she had come to announce she was quitting for the day. But her pallor didn't go with anything so mundane.

She faltered, 'Dev, I—'

An arm thrust her aside, and George, the Huffaker chauffeur, staggered into the room, his feet moving as though they were in lead boxes. His spoiled handsomeness had been that of a statue worked over by an interested but incompetent sculptor. Now, though, he wasn't a statue. He was a prizefighter who had walked into a round full of trouble and was valiantly hanging on for the bell. Sweat streaked his features, and breathing seemed to be agony. As though I were the trainer waiting in his corner, his eyes sought me feverishly. He was wearing a three-button jacket, and it was fastened, but blood was beginning to seep through from his shirt, the whole front of which was soaked with it.

He said huskily, 'That crazy sonofabitch, Devlin—'

I was immobilized behind my desk. He made gestures

like a marionette, and before I could get to him, he went down with no more sound than the average forest-giant being felled for the sawmill.

I got out fast from in back of that desk. I knelt down beside him while Sue cowered tearfully near the door. The bullet was lodged just below his heart, and I suspected it had found the lung. I wouldn't have counted myself an expert on gunshot-wounds, but from the look of this one and George's speech and appearance, I felt pretty sure he was a goner.

One hell of a plucky one, though.

Wondering how far he had walked and driven, I knew the trip couldn't have done him any good.

But he had done it for her, I knew without asking. And he had come to me—and not, I was convinced, merely to look at a friendly face.

Because his eyes were closed, I slapped him. I would have time to feel ashamed about that later.

'Come on, George,' I pleaded harshly. 'Don't crap out on me now. Who did this? Who was it?'

He opened his eyes, greeting me with a grotesque grin of pain.

'It was Huffaker,' he said. 'That crazy bastard.'

'Where? Tell me where.'

'The house.'

'Was Hartman there?'

'No.' He told me the rest in short bursts punctuated by agonized gasps, the speech of a man reaching for a rope paying out too fast for him to clutch at it for long.

'Huffaker's out of his skull. Came in waving a gun. Drilled me when I tried to take it away from him. The bastard killed Mrs Huffaker. Ran out saying he was going to get Hartman. Tried to call him, Devlin—warn. No answer.'

His hand groped for my wrist, found it and gripped it urgently.

'Take it easy, George,' I said. 'I'll warn Hartman. The cops will pick up your boss.'

As though I were wilfully misunderstanding him, he shook his head impatiently.

'Something else,' he hissed. 'Somebody tipped off Huffaker.' He shook his head wearily and, his voice thick with blood, added, 'That poor . . .'

He died before he could finish it, but I knew what he had been trying to say—'that poor lady'.

The predictable last thought of a faithful watchdog.

Automatically, I felt for his non-existent pulse. But the superfluous action was just a gesture.

I stood up slowly. Sue was still near the door, shaking and horrified.

'He's through,' I said. 'He was paid for his services, but he donated the sort of loyalty money can't buy. And then they talk about a servant-problem. Quite a fellow.' In a different tone, I asked, 'Are we alone?'

It had crossed my mind that by a stroke of bad luck someone else could have been in the outer office when George burst in.

Sue nodded slowly.

I stepped over the body and closed the door.

I gestured towards George. 'Overhear any of that?'

'A word here and there.'

'No, you didn't. Not one word.' She looked startled, uncomprehending, but I went on, 'We're going to have to get some law, but if I call them, I'm going to be up to the neck in the boys in blue for at least the next hour. I don't like that. So *you* are going to call the police. You didn't hear any of that conversation just now, because it didn't take place. George here crashed in demanding to see me, but I had left a few minutes before. He wouldn't take no for an answer. He thrust you aside and staggered into my office, where he collapsed and died. You never set eyes on him before, and that's all you know. At that, it's pretty close to the truth.'

She shook her head. 'I can't do it.'

'The devil you can't!' I poured her a stiff belt of Four Roses and shoved the glass at her. 'Drink that like a good girl.'

Like a good girl, she drank it. She drank it as though Prohibition were coming back tomorrow.

'Now listen to me. Al and I didn't hire you just because we like to look at your legs, attractive though they are. You are going to do this because you are competent, mature and self-possessed. You are going to do it because you know it won't blow up in your face. Most of all, you are going to do it because you have my promise that I shall shield and protect you. Are you going to do it?'

146

'Yes.' She nodded. 'Yes, I'm going to do it.'

I kissed her cheek and prepared to move out. I had all but gone when she said, 'Dev?'

'Yes, honey?'

'Sometimes I think you missed your vocation.' She made a brave attempt at a smile. 'If things ever get tough, you should try selling insurance.'

Chapter Seventeen

Things were getting tougher by the moment, I thought as I took the stairs down in order to reduce the risk of being remembered leaving the building. Conceivably, George, mortally wounded and bleeding, might have attracted attention, and I didn't want anyone telling the cops I had left *after* his arrival. They didn't like it if you didn't stick around to keep the corpse company.

That side of affairs didn't worry me too much, however. Sue would give a more than adequate performance, and George's demise, complicated only by his crawling into my office to die, was the sort of open and shut case the cops liked—inasmuch as they ever liked anything.

On the street, I spotted the Huffaker Rolls where George had left it, double-parked and with the driver's door improperly closed. The sight of the Rolls eliminated one possibility. Since I knew Charlie Huffaker only from his picture and long-range views of him outside his office and the Beverly Hills Hotel, I wasn't going to be able to identify him from the wheels he was driving—unless he had taken Yvonne Huffaker's Lincoln.

I climbed into the Olds and took off, burning up rubber with a sound that would have made me die of shame in less urgent circumstances.

The speed of events made instant analysis tricky, but George had set the tired Devlin computer whirring again. Who had tipped off Charlie Huffaker that his wife was zapping with Victor Hartman? One possible and obvious answer was Samuel Bishop, provided with the information by me. In some strangely misanthropic and meddling act, whose consequences he could scarcely have foreseen, Bishop had tipped off Huffaker and then committed suicide by blowing the top of his head and most of its contents all over the study.

I couldn't buy it. The more I inspected the picture, the phonier it seemed.

Using the number I had been given, I had called my client at the house in which Bishop had died that afternoon—true. I knew my client's voice, and it was he with whom I had spoken. But the dead man had been Bishop, and Bishop had not been my client. My client, then, lacked the obvious motive—if it really was obvious —for blowing the whistle on the liaison between Yvonne Huffaker and Victor Hartman.

It was crazy—all of it. And it was getting crazier by the minute.

Eight of those crazy minutes passed in my journey to Maple Drive. I tricked my way into the Rubidoux Apartments and made straight for Apartment 3C. On the way, I saw nobody, shadow or substance, who could have been Charlie Huffaker. Leaning on the door-buzzer produced no results, even when I added the extra touch of saying that I had a telegram for Mr Harkness. But without checking the garage, I could not be sure that Hartman was nowhere in the vicinity, and so I rode the elevator to the basement. Down there, a white Aston Martin would have been as easy to pick out as a great dane at a poodle-show.

No Aston Martin.

I debated what to do next. Strolling up the ramp, I checked the street. If Huffaker was lurking anywhere near the Rubidoux Apartments, I failed to see him. I asked myself whether it was likely that he would be there, but my attempt to get into the mind of a homicidal psychopath was abortive. Huffaker had committed two terrible, unthinking acts, but by now he had had time to cool and reflect. For all I knew, he might, stricken by remorse, already have given himself up to the police.

He might, but I couldn't take the risk that he hadn't.

Returning to the basement-garage, I was about to select a good place from which to keep watch when the white Aston Martin glided down the ramp, turned sharply and slid into one of the vacant slots. By the time I walked over, Hartman was almost out of the car.

He didn't know me, I was sure, but I was uncertain whether he knew *of* me. That depended on whether

Yvonne Huffaker had had time to warn him of my existence. From George's terse account, I figured there was a chance she hadn't.

At my approach, he stared blankly, but when I addressed him by name not using his pseudonym of Harkness, some expression of alarm showed in his eyes.

I didn't have time to inspect it.

Behind him, I saw what he, with his back to the phenomenon, could not see—a shadow which, in the half-darkness of the basement, rose from between two parked cars and began, like some avenging spectre, to point in his direction. We were close enough for me to hit Hartman, and I did, putting all my weight behind a right to his shoulder. With time short, the essential quality of the punch was speed, but it was well calculated, he was slimly built, his feet weren't set as they would have been in a fight, and he toppled backwards, his arms sprawling.

I threw myself after him, and sometime between the punch and my dive, a gun went off. There was a whanging sound as the slug found metal. By then, Hartman was on his back, and I was on top of him.

'Stay down,' I growled—an unnecessary exhortation, since my weight must have knocked the wind out of him.

I groped for my gun.

The man who had emerged so suddenly from concealment and fired, only to see his big chance spoiled, hesitated merely for a moment before he leaned forward again in a feral crouch, his right arm extended.

I was a stranger to him, but since I stood—or more

accurately lay—between him and Victor Hartman, so much the worse for me. However, I couldn't have formulated that thought until later, for as his bent arm thrust forward, I brought up my hand, the .38 in it, and fired.

Chapter Eighteen

One shot overrode the sound of the other so closely that they seemed simultaneous—as they very nearly were. Hartman and I, sprawled on the deck, were a difficult target, and our attacker missed. But I, too busy to aim, got lucky. The man cried out, staggered and clutched his right arm high up near the shoulder.

Perhaps more satisfying, I heard the clatter, too, as he dropped the piece.

Ignoring Hartman, I scrambled to my feet and ran the ten yards or so separating the man and me. He was just bending down to reach for the heater, a .38 automatic, with his left hand when I kicked it aside and shoved my own rod under his nose. He straightened up slowly. Devoid of boyish charm, the monkey-like features did not look amicable as they had done in the photograph, but I was unquestionably gazing into the darkly simian features, illuminated by obsessive eyes, of Charlie Huffaker.

I did not like the reports I had heard of him, I hated

what he had done and I was still shaken by what he had tried to do to me and Hartman. I was rough, my anger only just in check, as I grabbed him to inspect his wound. My bullet had nicked the flesh and was not lodged in his arm. As a disabling shot it was a beauty—the kind I would probably have missed if I'd had chance to take careful aim. He was not even bleeding profusely.

I put cuffs on his wrists, expecting some sort of verbal outburst. But there was none. Perhaps the tide of nihilistic furore had subsided, leaving him limp. If so, Huffaker revealed no sign of contrition or even mortal weariness at the enormity of his day's work. He was an interesting study, but the head-doctors could have him, and they were welcome to him.

My prisoner secured, I felt myself relax a little. When I turned around, Hartman was on his feet and had just finished dusting himself off. With an air of bafflement, he came towards me.

'I'm looking forward to a talk with you,' I said. 'Meanwhile, I take it you know our guest? If I'm wrong and you don't, this is Charlie Huffaker—Yvonne's husband.'

Hartman wasn't looking at me. In a flat voice, he said, 'You tried to kill me.'

When Huffaker didn't answer, I said, 'Yeah—well he's a trifle disturbed right now. Look, we need some law. Maybe we should all go upstairs and start sorting this out.'

Hartman finally looked at me and nodded slowly. The

dimensions of recent events seemed to have left him as
drained as his would-be killer. Perhaps it was just as well.
I didn't want the two of them at each other's throats,
with me in the middle, and with what I had to tell him, I
imagined a little protective numbness couldn't do
Hartman any harm.

I prodded Huffaker with the .38 and we moved
towards the elevator. When the car arrived, we rode upwards in a silence that I valued as a prelude to hitting
Hartman with the news he clearly did not know. I valued
it, that was, until I figured out there was no way of
picking my words with care.

I had expected a barrage of questions from Hartman,
but none came. Either he was an unusually disciplined
man or my diagnosis of shock was accurate. Huffaker
groaned once with pain, but said nothing. Apart from his
eyes, he didn't look like a homicidal nut, though such
paranoidal characters rarely did. I wondered whether he
was already thinking about consulting his lawyer and the
kind of defence they would prepare.

The hell with him.

Outside the door of 3C, we paused.

Hartman was uncomprehending until I murmured,
'The key'; and then he produced it, and we went inside. It was just a moderately comfortable furnished
apartment like thousands of others, and I speculated
about the basis on which he had chosen it.

But not for long. I shoved Huffaker down into a
chair, and then turned to face Hartman.

157

F

I said, 'You don't seem to know me, so perhaps I'm a stranger to you. I'm Brock Devlin, a private investigator. I came here to warn you because I knew Huffaker might try to kill you. How I knew that is going to be tough to explain and tough to hear. There's no way to build you up to this, so I won't be silly enough to try. Earlier this afternoon, Huffaker shot and killed Yvonne and mortally wounded George.'

Hartman didn't respond. A nerve twitched in his cheek, but he said nothing.

Huffaker did, though. He demanded, 'What is this? I thought you were the police. Now it turns out—'

'Shut up.' I leaned over him, waiting for an excuse to rattle his jaw. 'Shut your goddam mouth.'

He must have seen something in my eyes, because he fell silent immediately.

I returned my attention to Hartman, commenting, 'This is all kind of complicated, but if you get the complete news at once, at least it's quick. There's more to come. Your father committed suicide this afternoon.'

'My father?' he repeated.

Something was going on inside him, but I would have found it hard to say what. Grief and sadness were passive emotions. They were not feelings to inspect in Victor Hartman's eyes, where more positive processes seemed to be implied.

'Yes, your father—Samuel Bishop.' I muttered, 'Maybe you better sit down. I'm going to call the police.'

Turning my back on him, I began to dial.

158

Over My Dead Body

The telephone was alive. The juice from it streaked up my arm like fire, flashed through my nervous system and hit the back of my skull with a big yellow explosion. As its brilliance faded, I saw the dark swell rolling towards me—a ninth wave of blackness and oblivion. I was two people. One looked on dispassionately from the shore. The other, like a gull trapped in an oil-slick, made some vain effort not to slide under.

And then the wave engulfed me.

Chapter Nineteen

Victor Hartman's voice was at the bottom of an echoing airshaft, but he wasn't saying, 'You tried to kill me' in expressionless tones. He was talking sense. No, not sense. But he jangled the keys to sense.

They made a pleasant noise. It *was* pleasant—drowning and then feeling your cold corpse wash up on the warm shores of awareness, knowledge. But they shouldn't be warm. All that warmth and darkness were conducive to inertia, comfort, sleep.

Sleep, then.

No, no sleep for you, Devlin. Too easy. You wouldn't be happy. You're more at home being chased, shot at, beaten in alleys—the little things that mean so much.

Meaning . . . Concentrate, sucker.

'Mr Broderick, please . . . This is urgent . . . Yes, that's what I said . . . Ironic, isn't it? . . . Nothing to detain me now . . . Immediately, if I'm to avoid police involvement . . . Seven o'clock flight . . . '

The keys jangled. The voice came and went. The

carpet in my mouth tasted of dust and transients—anonymous people in an anonymous apartment. A pun there—dust and transience. Laugh, Devlin, laugh.

Eyes like windows with venetian blinds. Mighty tugs on the cord to draw them up. Then you can see feet. Feet moving, and a door opening and closing.

In a dream.

Your dream, Dev. Wake up.

No, sleep is fine. Schopenhauer had it right. Sleep is sweet. Death is better. But it would be best of all not to get born.

Sleep, then, sucker. Be a loser.

But wouldn't it be great, just for a change, to be on the winning side for once?

When I came round, about four minutes has elapsed, I had calculated. My head was the interior of a kettle-drum during Beethoven's Fifth Symphony. Nausea was lurking inside me, but I kept it under control. Hartman was gone. Charlie Huffaker was slumped in the chair, out cold and not dead, as I at first, with sickening thoughts of revenge, suspected. Hartman had sapped me as I tried to make my telephone-call. Then he had dealt with Huffaker.

I found the weapon on the floor—a heavy glass ashtray.

Victor Hartman . . . As if my head weren't enough, a lead weight started to roll around in my guts. My involvement was less personal, but I experienced what I

162

had felt when I once entrusted Kay to a deranged killer —a sense of appalling fallibility. Right facts, right theories, wrong man.[1]

My gun was on the floor, where I had dropped it as I collapsed. I retrieved it and staggered to the door without a clear plan, merely with the urgent instinct to find Hartman and end the mystery.

The elevator was at basement-level, presumably after Hartman had used it to ride down to his car. Leaning on the button, I thought that there was just a chance I might get to the Olds and beat him to Los Angeles International Airport.

The doors opened, but the car was not empty. Three tall, dark-suited, clean-shaven men were in it. They stepped out, and if you could say so of three pretty solidly built guys, they flowed round me, engulfed me and swept me away.

It was all over in seconds and almost without sound.

One moment I was about to take the elevator. The next, though no hand was actually laid upon me, I had been borne back by mere physical insinuation along the hall and into Hartman's apartment, where one of the men closed the door. Somehow, I didn't think of pulling my gun, perhaps because I had not been overtly threatened or molested.

Maybe, too, because I realized that three against one were long odds.

Taking a good look at the impersonally efficient trio, I

[1] *See* Dead on Arrival

decided I had never seen any of them before.

Three more strangers with persuasive ways.

One of them said, 'If you don't mind, I'll trouble you for the gun.'

Before I could move, he stepped closer to me and relieved me of it with deft movements that said he had done this sort of thing before. He also found Huffaker's gun, which I had dropped into a pocket.

'Why don't you sit down?' he suggested.

'Sure, let's get comfortable.' I sat down. 'You better do something about our friend here before he wakes up. I've seen him in action, and he's deadly.'

They said nothing to that. Maybe they thought the cuffs on Huffaker's wrists were sufficient restraint. They stood facing me and stared emotionlessly at me. I didn't like that.

With such interchangeable types, it was difficult to pick out a leader, but I said to the one who had disarmed me, 'When do I get to see the big fellow?'

'Big fellow?'

'Sure—you know. The one who calls himself Bishop when the fancy takes him and is going to have to think up a new alias on account of the rightful owner of that name dealt himself out—permanently.'

No response.

Not immediately. These guys were well trained.

Then one of them whispered something to another, who left us after nodding.

'That's better,' I said. 'I always like to deal with the upper echelons.'

They were not to be provoked to comment, and their professional impassivity interested me. Some cops had that sort of resistance to goading. Also some FBI and CIA agents.

Three minutes went by before the door opened again. This time, the man I knew as Samuel Bishop came in.

No tinted lenses masked his eyes, which were dark and flat, peculiarly without depth. The grey, a cunning touch of make-up, had disappeared from his hair, with the result that he looked almost ten years younger. The facial twitches and contortions had been acting: he was another wooden Indian. But he was recognizably the same man and as tall as I had judged him to be in the back of the Mercedes.

I looked for the rings whose absence had revealed to me that the corpse I had inspected at the Bel Air mansion was not that of the man who had hired me.

He was wearing them on those elegantly manicured hands in which he presumably took so much pride.

He gave no sign of recognition, but whispered something to the three stooges. For whispering, we were doing better than a cathedral. Two of the men picked up Huffaker's still limp form and carried it out like somebody's laundry while the third held the door. Then he closed it, leaving me and his boss alone.

I recognized the symptoms. We were off the record—no witnesses.

Chapter Twenty

'Nice to see you again, Bishop,' I remarked. 'Or what name are you using today?'

'Names aren't important, Devlin.' Leaning against the door, he folded his arms in a classic pose of indulgent omniscience. 'Let's not worry about them.'

'No? But I do worry about them. Almost as much as I worry about affiliations.'

'Affiliations?' he smiled. 'These ten-dollar words throw me.

'Yes, affiliations. Belonging to somebody or something. An organization, for example. Like the CIA.'

There was no reaction, and yet there was a curiously eloquent quality to his immobility.

'You see,' I said, 'it took a while, but I got there in the end. I usually do. Yes, you and your subordinates are CIA or at least some sort of government agency involved in espionage and counter-espionage.' Though not so much as a muscle twitched, his stillness implied a threat.

'Don't worry. Whatever I say in this room, I don't expect you to confirm or deny a word of it. Not intentionally, anyway.'

'That's good. I'd hate you to be disappointed.'

'You don't mind if I talk, then?'

'Talk away. I'm afraid we have to detain you for a spell.'

'In that case, if it will while away the time, I'll try to be entertaining. Let's start with Victor Hartman, about whom you must know far more than I have been able to guess. Hartman is more than an electronics genius. He's also a disaffected intellectual, a disillusioned man who doesn't like the way this country is run. Despite the stuff you fed me, he's probably a walking computer, and you knew he was ready to defect. But here's the kicker—you *wanted* him to defect. The computer, I have to presume, has been programmed with useless information that will keep his host-country on a false line of research for months. Either that, or Victor Hartman is some sort of double-agent—though I find that more difficult to believe. Anything is possible, nevertheless, in this game. So here's Hartman all ready to go, closely in touch with an enemy contact called Broderick, when the boom gets lowered. Hartman falls inconveniently in love and starts stalling because he wants a reluctant Yvonne Huffaker to join him in his flight to the East. Incidentally, I'll never, of course, be sure of how much she knew, but he probably told her comparatively little of his motives. Anyway, the situation is enough to make a cat laugh. Both sides are wanting Hartman to take off—he even wants to clear out himself. But he's hooked on Yvonne Huffaker, who has good reasons for not wishing to become an expatriate of any kind.'

'You're a mean man with the guesswork, Devlin.'

'I could be as much as thirty per cent wrong—no more.' His contemptuous smile got to look a shade artificial. 'You were in a bind—how to give Hartman a shove in the right direction without tipping your hand either to him or to Broderick? Somebody—maybe you, because this seems to have been your baby—dreamed up the idea of a catalyst, introducing an ingredient to speed up the process of Hartman's departure.' I laughed at my own vocabulary. 'Catalyst is a polite word. You wanted a patsy, and you picked me. Why the little bit of detective-work? Because you fought shy of systematic close surveillance, figuring that Hartman and Broderick were bound to spot it sooner or later and that Broderick, if not Hartman, might get around to asking why you were holding off, why you didn't pick up our boy before he could skip. If I've guessed that you wanted Hartman to defect, Broderick and his employers, equipped with the same facts, could surely do likewise. One man, though, a private investigator who didn't even really know why he had been hired, was a different matter. He could easily provide the shove that was needed—especially if he got rumbled. Hartman, if the plan succeeded, would leave the country with everybody except those in the know believing that he had just got out in time. Why should I be picked as the PI?' My tone grew bitter. 'Because I was honest but, the way you saw it, dumb. On my last big case, I was duped, badly deceived. Just the sort of chump you were looking for. You figured that if I was that clumsy, Broderick would spot me and pull Hartman out, maybe with or without Hartman's co-operation, because Broderick must have been getting pretty impatient, too. You figured that if Broderick laid hands on me, I would be stupid enough to tell a convincing story about Bishop's concern. You were wrong on all counts.'

I paused, and he lit a cigarette. Though his hands were steady, I found the gesture significant. What I expected to get out of him was not words—at least, not many of them. He was too disciplined to say much when silence was his strongest weapon.

And not simply *his* silence. He must have been worrying about what, in the long term, to do with me.

I went on, 'While I'm mentioning Bishop, let's get something else clear. He had to be in on this—working with you.'

'Oh?'

'Yes. It doesn't stack up any other way. What puzzles me is his attitude in this, but maybe it's not such a puzzle. I'd put him down as a right-wing American of the most reactionary WASP kind, and you sure as hell played him that way yourself. You used his identity, his car and his telephone-number. You couldn't have borrowed so much

170

without his willing co-operation. But you started to make mistakes from the start.'

'Mistakes?' There was irritation in his voice. 'What sort of mistakes?'

'Little ones, subtle ones. But they began to build up and form a picture. Anxiety tipped your hand. The chemistry of the situation was such that you wanted fast results. You asked me once too often whether Hartman knew I was tailing him, so that I began to consider the strange possibility that you *wanted* him to know. You made the stimulating mistake of calling me at my apartment. That's an unlisted number that I give out to very few people, and in the interests of privacy, I change it every few months. Once you'd called me at that number, I began to consider that my client had even more pull than I would have expected Samuel Bishop to have. Then it suited your purposes to keep me clear of Acme, a logical area of investigation—that was a mistake. To balance it, you gave me one genuine line of inquiry—Ben Craddock. And Craddock made several shrewd comments about Hartman's character and expressed something even more valuable—surprise at Deborah Hartman's continued presence in LA. Though I couldn't fit that in until later. Time was against you, and you wanted me to find Hartman in a hurry. So you gave me a fake angle in the phoney Deborah, who steered me, as she had been instructed to do, straight to Victor. By the way, I offer you both my compliments as actors. If ever you give up this line of work, Hollywood ought to be interested. But the fake Deborah made a mistake, too, and I detected her in it immediately. The real Mrs Hartman is something of a lush, but the woman I saw at Ventura mixes some very weak drinks to get loaded on. If it's any consolation, though, her performance was so brilliant I'm still not sure whether Bishop was Hartman's father or whether that was just some inspired improvization. I sure hope nothing bad happened to that gifted lady.'

'Nothing bad?'

'Sure.' I could be as faux-naif as he could. 'There was some shooting out there. Maybe Broderick hired some men to pay her a visit. Anyway, after it was over, there was a fast cover-up job, but I dug a slug out of one of the walls. It was after that second visit that I checked to discover the real Mrs Hartman has been back East for a long time. While we're talking about them, your cover-up jobs were too fast and too thorough. Except when they had to, your boys may not have moved in close, but they were always around. Pros like me and my partner develop a sense for things like that. We couldn't prove it, but we could smell their presence. If I hadn't already been thinking along those lines, that set me speculating about a big outfit with large resources of men and equipment. It figured—especially when that Mustang disappeared. That was your boys, wasn't it?'

'Devlin, I—'

'I know. You're not going to confirm or deny anything. One feature of that episode bothered me—some small detail I had overlooked. Later, I remembered what it was. I recalled the sound of a helicopter that I had been too busy to worry about. It was overhead, though, hovering not too far away. Your people, I suppose. In the time you had, it was relatively easy to spirit that Mustang away, either by lifting it or setting down some beefy guys to right it and drive it away. Unlimited funds and men can perform miracles. Like when I must have worried you by getting too close to Broderick—another small miracle. Your men jumped me to allow him to escape.' I laughed. 'Unless they were *his* men. In so tricky a game, it's hard to tell the good guys from the bad guys.'

He glanced at his watch, and slight though the movement was, I detected it.

'I can't be that boring,' I commented. 'Ah, I get it. You're waiting for the news that Hartman is safely tucked away on that flight to—where? Berlin, maybe? Farther east?'

His reply was suave and thoughtful. 'I made a big mistake about you. The way you're talking is bitter, Devlin. I hope you're not going to be trouble.'

'Trouble? Me? Hell, no. But, then, you know how to handle trouble. Like the way you handled Bishop's suicide. I take it his death *was* suicide, since it's hard to see how it fits into your plans. Damned inconsiderate of him to knock himself off, and particularly just then. If I wasn't off the case already,—and I was, though it's just possible you didn't know that—then his demise dealt me out. But you had a smart notion. Why the hell didn't you dream of it sooner? You provided the final shove by tipping off Charlie Huffaker that his wife was making it with Victor Hartman. It worked better than you could have expected, even though things got a little out of hand at that point. Death for two people, of course. Tragedy for Victor Hartman. But, hell, that's blood under the bridge. These minor events can easily be accommodated in the theory of historical costs. It's an obliging theory.'

Whoever he was, he reminded me of a movie-actor I had once known who had retreated into a dream.[1] Only with this man it wasn't a dream but a series of stratagems divorced from my outmoded squeamishness—the system.

Throughout all I had said, he had seemed little more than politely interested, concerned only with how I could be handled, not with the ethical considerations that might have disturbed a different sort of man. I wondered when he had last indulged in such kid-stuff as soul-searching and the endless soliloquy of scepticism.

Not lately, I imagined.

He and I were separated by much more than the answers he knew and I would never know. For all that he was years older than I was, he belonged to a newer America—the America of the wire-tap and the elaborate double-cross, of Watergate and the secret dossier and official, sanctioned blackmail, the America in which the means had finally become the end.

He was a twentieth-century man, and I wasn't sure where that left me.

[1] *See* The Girl in the Wet-look Bikini

Just then, the door opened, and one of the wooden Indians poked his head around it. He whispered something to my audience, who failed to suppress an expression of satisfaction. The door was closed again.

Chapter Twenty-one

Guessing the news, I said, 'So our boy made his flight without mishap. Well, there was no reason why he shouldn't. He could see my information was genuine, and mad Charlie more or less corroborated it. Poor Victor. There was nothing to detain him any longer, and he knew it.' I touched my scalp tenderly. 'You know, it's funny. I don't even feel sore at him for a crack on the back of the head he gave me.'

'You are sore, though. More of a hothead than I would have believed.'

'Let me worry about my disposition. Expediency is your preoccupation.'

'There you go again with the ten-dollar words. It must be contagious.'

'—Living with a writer.' He didn't actually say the words, but I picked up the implication out of the air.

'Right,' I said. 'Beat-up PI's aren't supposed to keep company with gifted writers, though there's no law against it—yet. You're probably working on it, though.

177

You know, you do your research well. What else do you know about me?'

'That you're an angry man. And that's not research.'

'So?'

'Before you walk out of here, I want some sort of guarantee that you'll keep your mouth shut. I'm old enough to be a judge of character, and it's my opinion your word will do.'

'That's big of you. But I'm not giving my word.'

'You have a certain nuisance-value, Devlin, but you admit there's little you can prove. Shooting your mouth off could make you look pretty silly.'

'Maybe. But I have to do something—if I can.'

'Licences can be revoked, Devlin.'

'Threats? I'm flattered.'

'But not impressed. Not yet, you're not. But you may be.' His mouth, never very attractive, now looked unambiguously ugly. 'I may not turn you loose.' He nodded. 'I could do it. I have the power. In the interests of security.'

'I'm convinced, but I'm not scared. You see, I have some power of my own. I've been keeping notes on this case, a sort of diary—names, dates, times, places, even theories and suppositions. You'd be surprised how up-to-date that account is. You could swoop on my apartment right now, but you'd be too late. You might pick up one copy, but there are others. Three? Four? More? You guess. And where are they? My attorney? Safety-deposit box? A newspaper-office? All you know for sure is that if **anything** happens to me, that story hits the fan.'

He took one last drag from his cigarette and screwed it out.

He said, 'All right. It's a stand-off. We leave you alone, and you keep your mouth shut.'

'I didn't say that. What I am saying is that I walk out of here in a couple of minutes, and neither you nor your men will lay a finger on me. There are no guarantees. Whatever I do is up to me and my conscience—if you'll forgive that old-fashioned word.'

'I don't get it.' He looked puzzled. 'What's with you? Why are you so sore?'

'If you have to ask the question, you wouldn't understand the answer.'

'You were paid well.'

'It's not money.'

'You have the knowledge that you served your country—'

'Don't give me that crap. Don't tell me how old you are and how much you've seen. The interests of my country are debatable, to say the least. If I served them, I didn't do it willingly or knowingly.'

'So that's it.'

'Yes, that's it. Two people died unnecessarily this afternoon—'

'That was an accident.'

'Only the dying. The rest you did. Now maybe you weren't to know that an insanely jealous husband would start throwing lead around, but you used him, just the same. Very civilized.'

'I haven't admitted that.'

'You don't have to. You did it. And you used me. I don't like that, and I don't like you. I don't like being manipulated. I hate people who tinker with other people's lives.'

'Ease up, Devlin. I did what I had to do. Security demands sacrifices, even of those unwilling to make them. Look at it this way. Without a vigilant government, that civilization you seem to prize so much would perish. I'm not saying anything goes. But sometimes the need dictates the method. Think it over.'

'Is that so? Well, I won't debate with you. But I'll let somebody else do it for me. Just now you pretended to find my literacy pretty funny. You could be right, but I try to wear it at a rakish angle. Anyway, I read probably more than is good for me. I read, and I remember. Like a few words from Walter Lippman. They seem to fit. "It is in the countless realms of privacy that civilization is carried on. Were it not for those ultimate reserves of private habit, energy and adaptability, the failures of the rulers of men would long since have proved to be irreparable." '

There was a pause. Then he shook his head and even managed a small smile, like the sun making a token appearance on a winter's day.

He remarked, 'Never trust a man with so small a stake in society. I prefer family-men. They're easier to persuade. You're one of a kind, Devlin. I'll say that for you. Out of all the cheap peepers we could have used, I have to pick you. They told me you were honest, but I didn't realize you were rotten with integrity.'

'Yeah,' I agreed. 'It's tough all round.'

'Perhaps not that tough.'

'No, maybe not.' I inclined my head in acknowledgement of his impregnability. 'Maybe I can't fight you, but I'm damned if I'll play your game. I'm through talking. Stand aside, please.'

'Why not?' He opened the door for me and even gave me back my gun. 'You're free to leave. With that gaudy luxury of yours.'

'Luxury?'

'Conscience, Devlin. It has no place in this century.'

As I went out, he didn't seem unduly perturbed—a lack of emotion that was scarcely surprising. I didn't even know his name, let alone who paid his salary. All I had was uncorroborated testimony. He and his men might have broken a law here and there, but I would have a hell of a job proving it.

I could do nothing for the dead. Principle might be important, but I inhabited a world devoid of villains and heroes. A part of me wanted to believe that Victor Hartman had acted out of principle, not for baser motives.

But Hartman's morality was ambivalent, the sort that could have a tired PI drowning in metaphysics.

I nodded to the man I had known as Bishop. I knew that I would never see him again—never see any of them again.

As I rode the elevator to street-level, though, I thought that I would sleep better than he would.

Crap! Sentimental hogwash.

Any guy who looked you in the eye and told you he did what he had to do would sleep at least as well as you did. He was shut off from your doubts, your ethical question-marks, your infinite scepticism.

They said the smog was bad that month. It seemed to me they exaggerated. As I left the Rubidoux Apartments, I quickened my step, and it felt good to breathe fresh air again.